everyday angel

Last Wishes

Also by Victoria Schwab

Everyday Angel #1: *New Beginnings*
Everyday Angel #2: *Second Chances*

VICTORIA SCHWAB

everyday angel

Last Wishes

SCHOLASTIC INC.

ISBN 978-0-545-52848-1

12 11 10 9 8 7 6 5 4 3   15 16 17 18 19 20/0

Printed in the U.S.A.   40
First edition, January 2015

Book design by Yaffa Jaskoll

chapter 1

MIKAYLA

Mikayla Stevens was made of gold.

That's what Miss Annette was always saying, but tonight it was true. She was wearing a gold leotard, and her dark skin was dusted with glittering powder — every time she rubbed her face, some came off on her hand. She considered her reflection in the mirrored wall, and realized she looked like one of those figurines they put on the tops of trophies.

Only gold girls go to Drexton, she recited to herself. But as her gaze drifted down from her face to her body, she cringed, taking in the catalog of imperfections: She wasn't tall enough. Her legs were too short. Her waist wasn't that narrow. *Stand up straight*, Miss Annette would say. *Legs together*.

She forced herself to stand tall and smile. A practiced smile. A *winning* smile.

Halfway down the same wall Mikayla's classmate, Sara, was warming up on a barre. Sara was a foot taller than Mikayla, long-limbed, and rail thin. She wore a shimmering green leotard, her blond hair pulled back in a perfect bun. The younger members of the Filigree Dance Company were across the room, a huddle of eight- and nine- and ten-year-olds, rehearsing their group number.

Only Sara and Mikayla were competing in solos.

The practice room was loud and full of dancers from across the region — ranging from little kids all the way up to teens, some in simple leotards, others in more ornate costumes (Mikayla envied those, even though Miss Annette said they were a distraction from talent), all waiting their turn to take the stage. A banner above the door read NORTHEAST DIVISION REGIONAL CHAMPIONSHIP.

"Five minutes, girls!" Miss Annette called, crossing her arms over a glitzy Filigree Dance Company sweater. Sara would be performing first, followed immediately by Mikayla.

Panic fluttered through her, the way it always did before she went on stage. Her stomach coiled nervously. She knew her dance routine backward and forward and upside down. She knew it inch by inch, and second by second, so it should be perfect.

It *had* to be perfect.

"Filigree dancers," trilled a voice through the intercom. *"Sara Olbright, Mikayla Stevens."*

The room snapped back into focus as Miss Annette gave a definitive clap and ushered Mikayla and Sara out of the room and down a hall toward the stage.

"Good luck, Sara," said Mikayla.

The other girl gave a thin smile. "I don't need luck," she said, heading toward the darkened backstage area. Mikayla reached for the door, but Miss Annette put a hand on her shoulder and crouched to look her in the eye.

"I don't want silver," Miss Annette said sternly. "And I don't want bronze. So what do I want?"

"Gold," replied Mikayla.

Miss Annette smiled, her teeth unnaturally white. "Exactly." She straightened and gave Mikayla a push. "I know you won't disappoint me."

Mikayla swallowed and nodded while Miss Annette scurried off into the audience to grab a seat.

When Mikayla snuck a peek through the velvet curtains, she could see the judges at their long table, the trophies beside them, the cash prizes in elegant envelopes beneath. She *needed* to win. Her parents needed her to win.

Behind the judges sat the audience, a mass of families and friends and coaches and dancers who'd already gone and were waiting for the awards at the end. Mikayla's mom was out there somewhere, filming on her iPad. Sometimes, Miss Annette told them, there were scouts in the audience, too. Mikayla had seen a poster one time that said DANCE LIKE NOBODY'S WATCHING, but Miss Annette said that was ridiculous; someone important was *always* watching.

Mikayla's pulse thudded in her ears. She closed her eyes, and tried to clear her head, but all she could hear was Miss Annette saying *gold gold gold gold*.

A routine ended, the music giving way to applause, and three cheerful girls bounded offstage, arm in arm, in matching blue outfits.

Sara stepped through the curtain, let out a breath, and disappeared onto the stage. The audience went silent, and the music began, and Mikayla put away the voices and pulled herself together.

She was up next.

chapter 2

ARIA

The shadow took shape on the curb outside.

It appeared out of nowhere, tucked in the dark between two streetlights. Everyone was inside watching the dancers, so no one saw the shadow grow or fill with light. No one saw the trace of wings above the shadow's shoulders. No one saw a twelve-year-old girl with curly red hair and a blue charm bracelet rise out of the brightened shape. And no one saw the girl tell her shadow, "Good job," and tap her foot until the light went out.

No one *saw* Aria step out into the world, but there she was. In a new place for the third time.

The last time.

Aria felt a rush of excitement. One more girl, one more mission, and she would finally have her wings. And then . . . Well, Aria didn't know what would happen after that.

5

First things first.

She exhaled, marveling as her breath made a cloud in front of her. She brought her hand to the fog, which fell apart before she could touch it. How strange.

It was much colder here than the last place she'd been, and she shivered and pulled her coat close around her before she even realized she was *wearing* a coat. She also had on jeans, a sweater, and brown boots. After a moment, she turned the boots a pretty shade of purple, and smiled.

In the distance there was a beautiful skyline: a cluster of tall, skinny buildings stretching toward the sky. A *city*. Aria had never been to a city before, and she was excited to explore.

And then Aria heard music. It was coming from the building to her right. She turned to look. A sign outside the building announced that the Northeast Division Regional Championship — whatever that was — was going on inside. Aria headed for the door; she could tell in her bones that this was where she was supposed to be.

Inside, the lobby was filled with boys and girls hurrying around in strange outfits, but none of them were marked by the blue smoke Aria knew to look for. Glitter and makeup and gossamer, yes, but no smoke.

The music was coming from an auditorium, and Aria nudged the door open and slipped in. It was crowded, so crowded that Aria worried she wouldn't find whomever she was looking for. A few hundred people sat in the audience, some in costumes and others in normal clothes, while on stage a blond girl in a green leotard was dancing. The girl was tall and thin, and her motions were elegant in a practiced way. Aria watched her leap and turn and tumble across the stage, landing on one knee just as the music ended. The audience applauded, and so did Aria, scanning the room for a wisp of blue smoke. Nothing. The girl on stage curtsied, looking pleased with herself, and then scampered off into the wings. A panel of judges sat at a table in the front row, scribbling on their papers.

And then the crowd grew quiet again. Aria's gaze drifted back to the stage, and she saw her.

The girl was pretty, her dark skin dusted with glittery makeup, and her black hair pulled back into a bun and tied with a gold ribbon. She was dressed in a shimmering gold leotard with a simple gold frill of skirt, and she sparkled from head to toe beneath the auditorium lights.

The only thing that didn't match her outfit was the ribbon of blue smoke coiling around her shoulders.

Aria straightened up at the sight. This was her. The girl Aria had to help. The last girl.

No one else in the audience could see the blue smoke surrounding the girl. But Aria could, bright and clear. It was the same color as Aria's charm bracelet, and her hand went to the third and final loop that hung on it. Waiting. The only loop without a feather on it.

Aria smiled, and the spotlight above the dancer brightened.

The girl struck a pose, draped backward like a flower, so far that Aria was sure she'd lose her balance. But the girl didn't. Even the smoke twisted around the girl with an elegant grace.

Then the music started, and the girl began to dance.

She was small, but when she danced, she seemed to fill the stage. Aria watched her carefully, in awe of her talent. There was something mesmerizing about the girl, the way she moved, like an extension of the music. Aria had to remind herself that the rippling smoke wasn't part of the routine, that it was being caused by something in the girl's life.

But what?

The girl's face was a mask of calm, but there was a moment — a fraction of time — when she closed her eyes and a small, private smile found its way onto her face. In that instant, the blue smoke thinned. But it was only an instant, buried in the middle of the routine. When she came to a stop, draped in the exact same position she had started in, the smoke was thicker than ever.

The crowd applauded, the judges scribbled, and when the girl smiled again, it was a different smile. A stiff, practiced smile. She vanished backstage and Aria got up to follow. She couldn't exactly go up on stage, so she ducked and circled around, drawn to the girl by a simple tug, as if a rope were running between them.

She rounded a corner and found the girl leaning back against a wall, head down. She didn't look like the girl on stage anymore. The girl on stage had been proud, confident, in control. This girl looked miserable.

Aria was about to step toward her when a woman appeared.

"Mikayla," said the woman, who had the girl's same dark skin (minus the glitter) and the same bright brown eyes. Aria guessed it was her mother. "You were wonderful."

Mikayla, thought Aria. What a pretty name.

The girl looked up but didn't smile. "I missed the turn," she said softly.

"Which turn?"

"At the end. I was supposed to spin four times, and I only did three."

"Well, no one noticed."

"*I* noticed." Mikayla's eyes shone with tears, and her mom tsked and ushered her back toward the audience.

"Hey," said Aria to her as she passed. "You were really amazing out there."

Mikayla flashed her that same hollow smile. "Thanks," she said. But Aria could tell she wasn't really listening. Mikayla's mind seemed miles away as Aria trailed her into the auditorium.

The rest of the dancers were good — some *very* good — but none of them were as good as the girl in gold. So Aria wasn't surprised when she won first place for her category. The blond girl in green took second.

When Mikayla Stevens (they called her full name) got up to take the trophy, and the cash prize, her smoke got even denser. Aria frowned, confused. The girl had won. What was making her so upset? Aria squinted at the smoke, as if she could see the problems in it, but all she saw was Mikayla's gold form beneath a blur of blue.

chapter 3

MIKAYLA

"There's my golden girl," said Miss Annette outside the auditorium, squeezing Mikayla's shoulder. "We'll work on that turn tomorrow."

Mikayla held the trophy to her chest, along with the check, and nodded.

The second-place trophy hung from Sara's hand. She held it with only the tips of her fingers, like she didn't want to touch it.

"What do you expect?" Miss Annette said to Sara. "It was a silver performance."

Sara's parents were standing nearby. They either didn't hear, or they pretended not to. Sara looked like she was about to cry. The rest of the Filigree girls were gathered around. The group routine had gotten bronze, but Miss Annette didn't seem to mind.

"Come on," said Mikayla's mom. "Let's get you home."

Mikayla pulled her Filigree Dance Company jacket on over her gold costume.

"Your dad wanted to be here tonight," said her mom, zipping up her own coat.

"I know." Mikayla's dad used to come to every event, back before he lost his job at the firm. Now it seemed like he spent every waking moment looking for work. She could picture him hunched over his laptop at their kitchen table, nursing a mug of coffee in one hand and furiously typing with the other, sending out résumé after résumé. He only left the house for interviews, and so far none of them had worked out. Her mom still had a job — she worked as a graphic designer for a small company. But she didn't make very much money, and it felt like their lives were tipping out of balance, about to fall.

"I filmed it for him, though!" Her mom waved her iPad. "We can all watch it when we get home."

On the way out, they passed that girl again, the redhead who'd told her she'd been amazing. The redhead smiled. Mikayla smiled back. There was something about her. Mikayla couldn't put her finger on it.

"I'm so proud of you," her mom was saying. "We should get a hot chocolate or something, to celebrate." Mikayla shook her head. She was already the shortest dancer in her bracket. She couldn't afford to put on weight. Not with the Drexton audition coming up. "What's wrong, M?" pressed her mom. "You just won, and you don't even seem happy about it."

Mikayla's smile must have faltered. She forced it back in place. "I *am* happy," she insisted. "Just tired."

The competition was outside the city, in New Jersey, so they'd had to drive instead of taking the subway. Now they climbed into the car and pulled away, the venue disappearing in the rearview mirror. They drove past a movie theater and a mall. Mikayla slumped back against her seat. She couldn't remember the last time she'd *seen* a movie, or gone shopping for something that wasn't for dance. A strange feeling twisted in her chest.

Her mom's cell phone rang. It was Dad.

"We're on our way home now," said Mikayla's mom, answering at a stoplight. "Yes, she was perfect." Mikayla cringed at the word. "Another gold. Yeah, I filmed it all. Okay. We'll see you soon."

The Stevenses lived in a townhouse in Brooklyn. It stood shoulder to shoulder with its neighbors, tall and thin, like a dancer, and made of pretty, dark bricks. Mikayla loved the house.

Which was why she hated the boxes. They hovered by the front door, and in the corners of the rooms, looming like shadows. A threat, a constant reminder that if her father didn't find another job, and soon, they'd be out of their lovely brownstone, crammed into a smaller apartment in a faraway neighborhood.

The boxes had shown up one at a time, throughout the house. At first her mom said she just wanted to clean up, clear out the things they weren't using anymore. Simplify their lives. But after she was done simplifying, the boxes kept coming.

"We have too much stuff," her dad said. "We don't need it." What he meant was, wherever they were going, there wouldn't be enough room.

"There's my girl," he said now, pushing up from the kitchen table. He looked tired but still threw out his arms, and she launched herself into the bear hug, the way she had when she was a kid. His arms still swallowed her up, made her feel small.

"Hi, Dad."

He pulled back and admired the newest trophy. "We're running out of space," he said, setting it on the table. Mikayla wondered if the trophies would be boxed up soon, too.

Chow, Mikayla's overly excitable spaniel mix, bounded up from under the kitchen table and leapt on Mikayla, licking her face. She giggled, feeling her spirits lift. By the time he was done, the dog's black fur was dusted with gold. Her mom let him out into the narrow back garden and began collecting her dad's coffee cups, which had multiplied.

Mikayla pretended not to see the bills stacked next to the coffee pot as she set the prize money silently beside it.

The first time she'd won after Dad had lost his job, she'd brought the check straight to him.

"Will this help?" she'd asked.

She hoped the sight of the money would make him happy, but, if anything, he looked more miserable than ever.

They'd always put Mikayla's competition winnings into a special college fund for her. But now she knew her *parents* actually needed the money. They didn't want to say it, as if by not saying the words out loud, they could somehow protect her from the fact that they were broke. But the truth was all around them. Just like the boxes.

"We can put it toward my Filigree classes," Mikayla had added, seeing her dad's hesitation as she held the check out to him. "That makes sense, right? Dance paying for dance."

"Okay," her dad had replied, reluctantly. "We'll put it toward Filigree. But only until the audition."

The audition. The only one that mattered. The one for the Drexton Academy of Dance. The most prestigious dance school in the city. Places rarely opened, auditions were once a year, by invite only, and every Drexton dancer was given a full scholarship. Enough to pay for the academy, for school, for competitions.

For *everything*.

Which meant she *had* to get in.

"So let's see this first place performance," her dad was saying now, nodding toward the iPad her mom was pulling from her purse.

Her mom propped the iPad up on the kitchen table and they all gathered around the screen as the video started.

Her parents beamed. Mikayla watched the gold-dusted girl take the stage. She looked like someone else.

Mikayla knew it was a good performance, but all she could see were the flaws. The mistakes that had cost her points. Yes, she'd won, but not by much. She could have lost. Could have taken second, which was the same as losing.

The judges had gone easy on her.

The Drexton committee wouldn't.

"I'm *so* proud of you, M," said her dad when it was over.

"So proud," echoed her mom. "Why don't you go change, honey, and then add this to the collection?" She gestured to the trophy.

Mikayla knew that was code for her parents needing to talk in private. Ever since her dad lost his job, they'd conversed in low, worried voices, and Mikayla could sometimes make out words like *costs* and *rent* and *benefits*.

Mikayla took her trophy and went to her room, changing out of her leotard and into stretchy pants and an old T-shirt. She scrubbed the rest of the gold dust from her face and undid her bun, finger-combing her thick dark hair. She could hear her parents' muffled voices in the kitchen.

Out in the garden, Chow was barking at something. Probably a squirrel. Chow was obsessed with squirrels.

With her trophy in hand, Mikayla slipped out of her room and padded downstairs to the basement.

For as long as she could remember, the basement had been her space. She'd played dress-up down here, watched movies with friends, made forts, and pinned up art. That was back when dance was just one of a dozen hobbies. Before it became the center of her life.

Three years ago, for her ninth birthday, the basement had been converted into a private dance studio, complete with a mirrored wall and a barre and shelf after shelf of trophies.

There were a few silver and bronze, but the vast majority were gold.

She set the newest trophy in one of the last open spots on the wall.

There were no boxes here. Not yet.

Next to the trophy shelves hung a wall calendar. On a date that looked dauntingly close, she'd written the word *Drexton* in red capital letters, a red circle drawn around it.

Mikayla rubbed her eyes, exhausted. But she turned toward the mirror and stretched. She raised her arms and started to spin, just as she'd done in the middle of the routine. Only this time she managed one, two, three, four turns before coming back to a stop.

She did it again.

One, two, three, four.

The shelves of golden trophies blurred as she kept her eyes on the mirror and spun, and spun, and spun, and stopped one turn shy, not because she'd messed up, but because something in the mirror had caught her eye. Well, not in the mirror, but in the window behind her. It wasn't a true window, not the kind you open or climb through, just a strip of glass near the top of the wall that looked out onto the grass in front of the townhouse. But she *thought*, for a moment, that she'd seen someone's face. Which was silly, because the face would have to be lying on the ground just to see her. Mikayla shook it off and lifted her arms again.

"Mikayla!" called her mom from upstairs.

She let her arms fall back to her sides. "Coming!" she called.

She cast a last glance back at the window, but of course, there was no one there.

chapter 4

ARIA

"That was close," whispered Aria to her shadow.

She had, in fact, been crouching on the ground in front of Mikayla's house, peering in through the tiny window into the basement below.

Aria had made it to the Stevenses' house before Mikayla (traveling by shadow was faster than traveling by car). She'd gone through the low gate and into the little back garden, but she'd been met with unexpected resistance in the form of a dog. The little barking creature had been able to sense her, even when she was invisible, so she'd come back out front. She'd let herself become visible again, and was about to wander away when she saw the light turn on in the basement window.

She'd crouched down, and watched Mikayla spin and spin and spin — she felt dizzy just watching her — and hadn't thought about the mirror or the fact that she was visible, not until it was too late.

She pressed herself back against the bricks, invisible again, and waited for the basement light to turn off. Then she looked up at the townhouse and wondered which room was Mikayla's, even though it didn't matter; she couldn't get inside, not without permission.

Just then, the front door opened, but it wasn't Mikayla; it was her father. He was carrying out the trash, but she could see past him into the townhouse and was surprised to see boxes stacked inside, as if they were getting ready to move. And then the dog — Chow, they'd called him — bounded out in the man's wake, and headed straight for Aria. He barked and wagged his tail and prodded her invisible knees with his wet nose.

"Good dog," whispered Aria.

"Chow!" snapped Mr. Stevens, dropping the trash in the can. He came over and picked up Chow, hauling the barking dog back inside and closing the door.

Aria let out a breath of relief and became visible again, an instant before a boy on a bike pulled up to the townhouse next door. He hopped down, took off his backpack, and tugged off his helmet. He had shaggy brown hair and blue eyes, and was roughly the same age as Mikayla.

He saw Aria standing there in front of Mikayla's house, and paused.

"Hey," he said.

"Hi," said Aria.

"You a friend of Mikayla's?"

Aria nodded. It was a small lie. And it wasn't so much a lie as an out-of-order truth, since she intended to *become* friends with Mikayla.

"I didn't think she had *time* for friends anymore." There was something in the way he said it. An edge, like hurt. "What with all the dancing." Aria didn't know what to say to that. "Sorry," the boy added, shaking his head. "That was harsh. I just miss her."

Aria smiled kindly. "What's your name?"

"Alex," he replied, locking his bike to the railing of the steps. "Well, tell her I said hi." And with that, he went inside.

Aria turned her attention back to Mikayla's house. She couldn't just stand around all night, waiting for morning or Mikayla. (Well, she could, but that didn't seem like a good use of time.)

So Aria started walking.

It was a cold night, but Aria wanted to see as much as she could. The single featherless loop on her bracelet whispered against her skin, a reminder that this was her last task, that everything that starts must end. It wasn't that she was afraid, exactly; she just didn't want to waste any time sitting still.

As she walked, she wondered about Mikayla Stevens — who she was, and why Aria had been sent to help her. She thought of the pieces of Mikayla she'd seen so far: the competition, the gold trophy — the *wall* of gold trophies — and her practiced smile. The moving boxes, and her father's troubled eyes, and Alex's comment on how she was never around. Aria wondered which thing was causing Mikayla's blue smoke, or if somehow they all were.

Whatever it was, Aria would find a way to help. She always did.

Meanwhile, the streets had quieted around her, but they still felt *alive*. There was a pulse to this place, an energy the other places she'd visited hadn't had. Aria liked it.

She walked on, her legs burning pleasantly, following the clusters of light that marked large buildings. She crossed a big circle, edged around a park that was sprawling and dark, and passed a massive stone building.

Then Aria looked up, and found herself standing in front of a large, curving gate. The gate was lovely, and covered in carved silver leaves, and bore the words BROOKLYN BOTANIC GARDEN.

Aria didn't know what *botanic* meant, but she knew what a garden was, and this one seemed impressive.

When she looked through the gate, she could see paths and trees, flowers and grass that seemed to go on forever.

The gate was locked, but not in the way that meant she had to be invited in. This place didn't belong to just *one* person or family. When Aria brought her hand to the gate, something clicked inside, and it fell open beneath her touch, just far enough for her to slip through.

Aria reached the edge of the entrance path, and her eyes widened.

Fairy lights hovered on the path, illuminating the gardens wherever she went. Many of the flowers had retreated against the chill, but as Aria walked past them, they blossomed again, pink and red and white and yellow.

"Isn't it wonderful?" she said to her shadow, and though her shadow never spoke, its head seemed to bob in the flickering light.

Everywhere she wandered, there was something new to see.

A field with trees lined up in perfect rows.

A lake with moonlight and lily pads floating on top.

A building made entirely of glass.

When she stepped inside the building, it was like walking into another world, the groomed gardens and cool fall air traded for a leafy green indoor jungle.

She couldn't think of a better place to spend the night.

The city, thought Aria, as she slipped back through the gate again around dawn, *is a magical place.*

Almost as magical as her.

chapter 5

MIKAYLA

WINNERS NEVER QUIT. QUITTERS NEVER WIN.

It was the first thing Mikayla saw when she opened her eyes each morning. The poster was taped to the back of her bedroom door, a pair of ballet shoes suspended beneath the words. It was one of Miss Annette's favorite phrases. She was full of sayings.

If it doesn't hurt, you're not trying hard enough.

You're only as good as your next dance.

Only gold girls go to Drexton.

Mikayla sat up, tired and sore. Her eyes traveled to the boxes in the corner of her room, then to the homework spread at the foot of her bed. She'd stayed up until midnight working on math problems but hadn't finished. She knew she had to keep her grades up if she wanted to stay at Coleridge.

Coleridge was the prestigious private school Mikayla had been going to since kindergarten. The prestigious private school her family couldn't afford anymore.

Mikayla had overheard her parents talking about it.

(Mikayla overheard her parents talking about a lot of things.)

Apparently Coleridge had agreed to give her a scholarship, so long as she kept her grades up. But it wouldn't take effect until after Christmas. By then, it might be too late. The Drexton audition loomed in her mind, more important than ever.

She got out of bed and went through her morning stretches, limbering her arms and legs, ankles and feet, working the stiffness out of her limbs. There was a floor-length mirror in her room, and she stood in front of it, assessing. Scrutinizing.

"Mikayla!" her mom called up the stairs. "Bye, honey. I'm leaving for work now. Don't be late to school!"

"I won't!" Mikayla called back. "Have a good day!" Her mom always left the house earlier than she did. There was a time when her parents would go to work together. Now, Mikayla knew, her dad was downstairs alone. At least he had an interview today.

Quickly, she showered, dressed, and packed up her school stuff, along with her Filigree dance bag. She swung the bag over her shoulder and grabbed a granola bar on her way out. Coleridge was located in Manhattan, just off the 3 line. Mikayla took the subway to school — she'd just been allowed to start taking it by herself.

"Good luck on the interview," she told her dad as she tugged on her coat.

"Thanks, hon," he said, looking as tired as she felt. *Please let him get this job*, she thought as she walked outside.

Next door, Alex was just swinging a leg over his bike.

"Hey," he said.

"Hey, she said.

Then there was an awkward pause, where they both opened and then closed their mouths. And then it was over. He waved and she nodded and he went off on his bike and she went off on foot.

Mikayla and Alex used to be inseparable, back when they were kids. She'd invite him over to build forts in the basement and he'd invite her over to play video games or go bike-riding in Prospect Park. And then at some point, Mikayla started saying no — for the same reason she said no to everything, because she had dance. And then, eventually, Alex stopped offering. They were still nice to each other, and she missed him, of course — sometimes on her way home from dance, she'd hear him laughing with friends in his backyard, or playing video games when the windows were open, and she wanted to join him — but dance came first. It had to. And besides, she told herself, they probably didn't have anything in common anymore.

She hurried down the steps into the subway station. The train was just pulling in, and she ran to catch it. It was already half-full, and she sank into a seat and pulled out the last of her math homework while the stops ticked past.

About halfway to Coleridge, she finished her homework and glanced up. A girl her age was sitting beside her. She looked familiar.

"Hi again," said the girl with a smile.

Mikayla frowned. At first, she couldn't figure out where she'd seen her before. And then it clicked. It was the redhead from the competition the night before.

"Hi," said Mikayla. "You were at Regionals last night."

The girl nodded.

"So you're a dancer, too?"

"I'm an Aria," she said.

"Like the music?"

The girl smiled. "No. Like the person."

"Oh," said Mikayla. "Well, hi again."

Aria swung her legs back and forth. She had on cute purple boots, Mikayla noticed. "Small world, huh?" she said.

Mikayla nodded, even though it wasn't really a small world. It was a big city, with millions of people. What were the odds that they'd bump into each other? "Where are you headed?" she asked.

Aria's gaze drifted down and landed on Mikayla's bag. There was a Coleridge School button on it. Aria brightened and pointed at it. "There!"

"No way," said Mikayla.

"It's my first day," said Aria, "so it's nice to know I'll know *someone*."

"Yeah," said Mikayla. What was it about this girl? She was open and chatty in a way that was out of place in the city. Mikayla had been taught not to talk to strangers. Aria looked like she would probably talk to anyone. It wasn't a bad thing. Just one more thing that made her stand out.

"What is it?" asked Aria, feeling the weight of Mikayla's gaze.

"It's just weird, crossing paths," said Mikayla. "You're not following me, are you?"

It was a joke, but the girl's eyes went wide and she looked nervous. "No . . . I mean, not really," she said. "Must be a coincidence. The world is full of those, you know. Unless you believe that everything happens for a reason, and then I guess maybe we were *supposed* to cross paths. What do you think?"

Mikayla shook her head, dazed. "I don't believe in fate," she said stiffly. "It just seems like an excuse for people who don't want to take responsibility for things." Her words came out harsher than she'd meant them, but it bothered Mikayla when people chalked things up to the universe. In dance, you were responsible for yourself. When you messed up, it wasn't because it was *supposed* to happen, it was because you failed to get it right.

"Well," said Aria cheerfully. "One way or another, I'm glad our paths crossed." She sounded like she meant it. Aria smiled, and it was crazy, but the train's fluorescent lights seemed to get brighter at that moment. Then Aria leaned forward, as if she had a secret. "You know, you really *are* an amazing dancer."

Mikayla felt embarrassed. "I could be better."

"Well, I hope so," said Aria, sitting back. "Wouldn't it be boring if you were already the best you could be? There'd be nowhere for you to go!"

Mikayla frowned. She'd never thought of it that way. But there *was* such a thing as *best*, especially when it came to competition. Mikayla turned to explain this to Aria, when she saw the girl gazing in awe at the subway map on the opposite wall. The train jerked forward and Aria swayed in her seat, crashing into Mikayla's shoulder. She apologized with a laugh.

"You're not from New York, are you?" ventured Mikayla.

Aria shook her head. "I just moved here."

"From where?"

Aria thought for a moment and then said, "California."

"Wow, that's a big change."

Aria beamed. "You have no idea."

Mikayla found herself returning the smile as she looked back at the subway map. She was so used to all the colorful lines and dots that she'd come to take it for granted. The train slowed, and she pushed to her feet, ready to elbow her way through the crowds. She glanced down at Aria.

"Come on! This is our stop."

chapter 6

ARIA

As they climbed the subway steps and emerged onto the street, Aria's mouth fell open.

The subway itself had been a new adventure — the not-terribly-pleasant smells on the platform, the passengers shoving and maneuvering around one another, the way the train snaked through the tunnels like a giant beast. But what waited for her on the other side was even more amazing. Brooklyn had been green and leafy and relatively quiet. This part of the city was stuffed full of dizzying skyscrapers, honking yellow cars, carts selling food, giant stores, and more people than Aria had *ever* seen. She looked around, mesmerized.

"What is it?" asked Mikayla.

Aria couldn't stop gazing at the city.

"It's *incredible*," she whispered.

Mikayla looked around, as if trying to see the streets and the people the way Aria did, but Aria knew she couldn't. To Aria, things were still strange and exciting. So many experiences were still foreign and new, which made the world a place of wonder and discovery. She wished more people could see life the way she did, could notice the things they'd gotten used to. She thought that if they could, it might make their lives a little more magical.

"Are you coming?" asked Mikayla.

Aria dragged her attention back to the girl and her blue smoke, and she nodded, determinedly.

"Have you always lived in the city?" Aria asked as they hurried down a busy street. She noticed how briskly Mikayla — and everyone else here — walked.

"Yeah," said Mikayla. "What about you? Had you always lived in California?"

Aria shook her head, thinking of the first place she'd visited, where she'd met Gabby. "No. I move around a lot."

"That's got to be hard," said Mikayla.

Aria shrugged. "I figure, I go where I'm supposed to be."

Mikayla chuckled. "You really do believe in fate and destiny and all that."

Aria chewed her lip. "I think there's a path. If that makes sense."

"Like the steps in a dance routine?" offered Mikayla.

Aria nodded. "Yeah. Sometimes you have to improvise, but I guess I believe there's a routine. A course things are supposed to take. So when it leads me to places, or to people, I assume I'm there for a reason."

Mikayla's brow crinkled, but she didn't say anything more.

At the end of the block, they rounded the corner, and there it was.

Coleridge School was a large brick building that looked like it had been there for a hundred years. The last school Aria had "attended," Caroline's school, had been very strict, with the girls in uniforms. Here, there was a mix of boys and girls, and no uniforms.

But everyone here, Aria noticed as she and Mikayla climbed the front steps, wore very *nice* clothes. The girls had on soft-looking creamy sweaters and jeans that fit perfectly. Velvety short skirts over patterned tights and shiny, brand-new boots. Luxurious-looking puffy coats. Mikayla, too, wore a pretty sweater dress with boots, but Aria noticed that her boots were a little scuffed, as if they weren't brand-new. Somehow, Aria could sense that this bothered Mikayla, even though Aria didn't understand why. She saw Mikayla glance down worriedly at her boots, then straighten up and adjust her smile until it was the perfect, practiced one.

"Mikayla!" someone called.

Mikayla waved and headed toward the voice, Aria trailing like a shadow.

Two girls were standing on the front steps, one with a tennis bag slung over her shoulder, the other holding a drawing pad to her chest.

"Hey," Mikayla said to the girls. She turned to Aria. "This is Beth," she said, gesturing to the girl with the tennis bag. "And this is Katie." She nodded toward the girl with the drawing pad. "This is Aria," she explained to her friends.

The girls, neither of whom had seemed to notice her yet — people rarely did, unless they needed her — smiled cheerfully. "Hey," they said in unison. And then they started chatting with Mikayla about homework and boys and a dozen other topics, all started and dispatched with lightning speed. Mikayla listened and nodded, and Aria wondered why she was wearing the practiced smile, instead of a real one.

And then the bell rang. Mikayla pointed Aria toward the main office. "If we're not in the same classes, then come find me at lunch," she said, before vanishing down the hall with Beth and Katie.

36

Aria hoped getting into Coleridge wouldn't be too hard. And it wasn't. Not with a little bit of magic. The man at the front office found Aria's name in the computer, with all the proper boxes already checked. Aria gave her best smile and was given a schedule in return.

She hadn't thought to arrange her schedule so that she shared classes with Mikayla. Still, she figured she might learn about the school and Mikayla's world by just attending the classes with the other students.

To her relief, Coleridge was pretty much like the two other schools Aria had been to. There was English, and history, and math. (Aria didn't like math, and she supposed she could just skip it, but that felt somehow like cheating.)

By lunchtime, Aria *had* learned a little bit about algebra, and about something called the Revolutionary War, and that a poem called "The Road Not Taken" was very beautiful. She'd also learned that all the Coleridge students seemed wealthy, but not all of them seemed snobby. But she wasn't much closer to learning what was behind Mikayla's smoke.

The cafeteria was huge and noisy, and she saw Beth and Katie sitting at a table with a few other girls, but no Mikayla. She scanned the room and saw Mikayla standing at the end of the lunch line, tray in hand, her blue smoke twisting thickly around her. She looked distracted. Aria wondered what kind of help the girl needed, and she knew she wouldn't find out by watching. So she grabbed a tray and headed over.

"Cookie for your thoughts?" she said cheerfully.

Mikayla blinked and looked up. For a moment Aria expected her to paste on that smile and say, "Nothing," but instead she said, "I can't remember the last time I went to a movie."

It wasn't what Aria had expected her to say. And she didn't know how to answer. She couldn't remember the last time she'd been to a movie either, because she'd *never* been to a movie.

"Beth and Katie were talking about this movie they saw over the weekend," explained Mikayla. "They're always going to movies. Plays. Concerts."

"So why can't you go with them?" asked Aria, setting an apple on her tray.

Mikayla sighed. "Dance," she said automatically, as if that was the answer to every question. "And money," she added, and as soon as she said it, she looked down at her tray and blushed furiously. Aria didn't see why Mikayla should be embarrassed (Aria knew that most people couldn't just magic money out of their pockets whenever they needed to). But Mikayla seemed upset. Aria thought of the boxes she'd glimpsed stacked inside Mikayla's front door and wondered if that had anything to do with the smoke. Or was it the fact that she was so hard on herself? That even first place didn't seem good enough?

In Mikayla's smoke, Aria could make out the edges of worry, and doubt, and stress, but it was all tangled, like a knot.

Aria opened her mouth to change the subject, but Mikayla was already heading for the checkout. By the time she led Aria toward a table where Beth and Katie were already sitting, she had that practiced smile back on her face.

As they were sitting down, Aria caught a glimpse of a familiar blond bun. Across the cafeteria was the tall, thin girl who'd won second place the night before.

"That's Sara," offered Mikayla.

"You two dance together, right?" asked Aria.

"We both go to Filigree," said Mikayla, as if the two statements were very different. "We usually walk there together after school."

"Speaking of," said Beth, taking a bite of her lasagna, "how were Regionals last night?"

"I did all right," said Mikayla, but Aria spoke up.

"I was there," she said, "and Mikayla was amazing. She won first place!"

Katie, who'd been doodling on her drawing pad, smiled.

"She always does." She sounded sincere, Aria realized, but there was something else in her words. A kind of sadness. Like she was proud of her friend, but also missed her, even though Mikayla was right there.

"Not true," said Mikayla. "Sara's getting better. If I'm not careful, she'll beat me."

Beth gave a dramatic gasp. "Because coming in second would be the end of the world!"

Mikayla managed a thin smile, but Aria could tell it was hollow, could tell that underneath the mask, beneath the perfect posture, the thought of coming in second was a horrible thing.

"Silver would clash with everything," said Katie thoughtfully. "We all know Mikayla only wears gold."

chapter 7

MIKAYLA

Mikayla had just left Coleridge with Sara, feeling the usual dread in her stomach whenever she had to spend time with the girl. They were halfway down the busy street, Sara listening to music through her earbuds, when Mikayla heard the sound of rushing steps behind her. She turned to find a breathless Aria catching up.

"Hey," she said. "Can I walk with you guys to Filigree?"

Mikayla's eyes widened. First the competition and then the subway and then Coleridge and now this? How could this Aria girl be everywhere?

Maybe we were supposed to cross paths. Aria's voice echoed in her head. Mikayla didn't believe in magic or things like fate, but even she had to admit this was getting weird.

Sara scrunched up her nose and tugged one earbud out. "Since when are *you* part of Filigree?"

"It's my first day," said Aria, apparently immune to Sara's attitude. She fell into step beside them. "Actually, that's why I was at Regionals last night."

"To scope out your competition?" asked Sara.

Aria frowned. "No," she said, earnestly. "Just to see you guys dance."

"Are you any good?" asked Sara.

Aria looked at her like she didn't understand the question.

"Of course she's good," said Mikayla, coming to her defense. "She wouldn't be coming to Filigree if she weren't."

Aria swallowed.

Sara shrugged, put her earbud back in, and cranked her music up. They were walking along Columbus Avenue. People were rushing past them, chattering into cell phones and holding coffees. They passed a hairdresser, a dry cleaners, restaurants with tables outside. Mikayla caught Aria looking around, so entranced by the city that Mikayla had to pull her out of the way of grumbling pedestrians. Twice.

"So," said Aria as they walked. "How long have you been dancing?"

Mikayla squinted, thinking back to herself as a chubby

little girl, in tights and a tutu for the first time. "Since I was five," she said. So it had been seven years. But sometimes it felt like forever.

"Wow," said Aria. "That's a long time. How often do you do it?"

"Six times a week." Back when she first started, she used to dance only twice a week, with foundations in ballet, jazz, and modern. But now her focus was contemporary, and somewhere along the way two times a week became four and then four became six. The only reason it wasn't seven was because Miss Annette took Sundays off. Now Mikayla felt like she was measuring dance not in times per week but in times per *day*.

It made her tired just thinking about it.

"You must really love it," said Aria as they stopped at a crosswalk. Sara stood beside them, lost in her music and cracking her gum.

"It's my life," replied Mikayla, feeling a strange heaviness when she said it. She forced herself to smile.

"So," said Aria. "What do you do when you're *not* dancing?"

Mikayla opened her mouth to answer, but nothing came out. She thought of Alex, and of Katie and Beth, and felt a pang of sadness. But she was spared from having to answer when they crossed the street and came to a stop in front of a small brick building. The sign on the front read FILIGREE DANCE COMPANY in bold, curving letters. "We're here," she said, dodging the question.

Aria looked suddenly very nervous. Mikayla brought a hand to rest on her shoulder. "You'll do fine," she said, trying to assure her. Sara had already vanished inside, and she started up the steps. When Aria didn't follow, Mikayla looked back. "You coming?"

Aria straightened, and nodded. "You go ahead," she said. "I'll be right behind you."

Mikayla went inside, surrounded by the familiar sight of mirrored walls and wooden floors, the familiar sound of music and Miss Annette's voice critiquing someone in a studio. But when she heard the sound of Aria at the front desk, she hesitated in the hall and listened.

"Can I help you?" Pam, the woman at the desk, asked.

"Hi, I'm Aria Blue. I'm here to join Filigree." Mikayla frowned. So Aria hadn't actually been accepted yet.

"I'm afraid we have a waiting list," said Pam. "You can't simply walk in."

"Oh," said Aria. "Sorry; I should be in the computer."

The click of keys on the keyboard, and then, "Sorry, you're not in here."

"Oh," said Aria again, sounding confused. "Can you check again? Aria Blue?"

"Sorry," said the woman after more typing. "No luck."

"Apparently not," said Aria. Mikayla chewed her lip.

"Filigree is a very competitive dance school," Pam said. "We can't exactly take on *everyone*. Admission is at Miss Annette's sole discretion. If you want to join, you'll need to audition."

"Great," said Aria, her voice brightening, "when can I do that?"

Pam started typing away again. "Hmm," she said. "Looks like the next opening is in just over three weeks."

"But I need to start now," insisted Aria. Mikayla didn't understand the urgency. Mikayla didn't understand what Aria was doing here at all, for that matter. It was starting to seem less like Aria had wandered into her life, and more like she'd marched.

"I'm sorry," said the woman, "Miss Annette is a very busy woman."

"Well," said Aria after a minute, "since I came all this way, could I at least join in today? I won't cause any trouble."

There was a long pause. "How much experience do you have?"

"I'm a very fast learner," she said.

The woman sighed. "Well, go get changed. You can stand in the back of the group lesson, and if Miss Annette has a few minutes, maybe she can fit you in. . . ."

Just then, Mikayla heard Miss Annette's voice boom out from one of the studios.

"What was that, Eliza?" she was shouting. "Was that supposed to be a ballonné? I can't even tell."

Mikayla heard Eliza's quiet apology, and she knew she better move quickly. Her own class was about to start. She hurried to get changed, nearly bumping into a beaming Aria outside the dressing room.

What are you doing here? Mikayla wanted to say. *Why are you here* now?

Instead she just said, "Do you have your dance clothes?"

"Of course," Aria replied, even though she only had a bookbag, not an extra dance tote like Mikayla did. But in the minute it took Mikayla to turn around and quickly change into her leotard, she looked back and saw that Aria was in a leotard herself. Mikayla didn't even know where Aria's school outfit had gone. It was as if the leotard had magically appeared. Weird.

46

Aria smiled, blue eyes bright. "I'm ready," she said. She turned to go, her red hair waving behind her.

"Wait," called Mikayla, pulling a hair tie from her wrist. She wrangled Aria's hair up into a ponytail, and then a bun, so it wouldn't get in the way.

"There," Mikayla said. "*Now* you're ready."

chapter 8

ARIA

Aria didn't know what had happened with the Filigree computer — she'd always been able to magic herself onto school rosters. She'd done it just that morning!

The only time her magic *didn't* work was when it wasn't *supposed* to (though she never knew what was allowed and what wasn't until she tried). So if she couldn't magic herself into Filigree, there must be a reason.

Or maybe her powers were just being ornery.

It didn't matter, she decided as she entered the classroom Mikayla had pointed her toward. Because she was here now. Standing in the back of a group lesson that was filled with eight- and nine-year-old girls.

Aria was a head taller than all of them, so she stood out like a tree in the middle of a garden.

Mikayla had gone into another studio, where Miss Annette taught the more advanced class.

In this one, a man named Clyde instructed the girls in Aria's group to do things like *chassé* and *pirouette.*

Aria had no idea what those words meant, but she'd told the truth to the woman at the front desk — she *was* a fast learner — and soon enough she was doing a half-decent job of keeping up.

"Jeté," instructed Clyde, and again, everyone but Aria seemed to know what that was. They lined up against the wall, and a small girl with a tight braid went first. She took a few fluid steps and then leaped high into the air. Aria watched in awe as the girl landed soundlessly on the wooden floor. She did three more flawless jumps, making her way to the opposite wall.

Aria felt suddenly very out of her element.

For a second she wondered if she should make herself invisible and duck into Mikayla's studio. But a good guardian angel didn't just watch. They became involved. They *intervened.* At least, that's what Aria told herself as the number of girls on her side of the room dwindled. She was secretly relieved that the other girls' jumps weren't all as impressive as the first girl's, but they were still *good.*

Soon it was just Aria against the wall, waiting.

Aria took a breath, and forced herself to go.

She took a step and then sped up. The wind whistled past her ears as she leaped into a jump. She stumbled as she landed, feeling clumsy.

"Try again," Clyde said, not unkindly.

Aria did. *Step, step, step, leap, split, land.*

She'd done it! It had actually felt nice, the sensation of being airborne for a moment. Aria couldn't fly, but this came close.

Aria smiled at the small victory. The fluorescent lights of the studio brightened.

When Clyde told them they could take a break, Aria turned to leave her studio to visit Mikayla's. But then the studio door opened and in marched an imperious-looking woman. Aria guessed she was Miss Annette.

"Clyde, I had a —" Miss Annette began, then paused when she saw Aria.

"What's this?" Miss Annette asked, scowling down at her.

Aria bristled — she was a *who*, not a *what* — but she managed to say, "I'm Aria."

"Where did you come from?"

"California," said Aria.

"And what are you doing here in my school?"

"I'm new. The woman at the desk said I could stay and that you might have time . . ." she trailed off under the woman's scrutiny.

Miss Annette gave her a long, head-to-toe look. "What kind of dancer are you?"

Aria wasn't sure how to answer that question. A new one, obviously. But she had heard Mikayla use the word *contemporary*, so that's what she said.

"Well," Miss Annette said. "Show me." The eyes in the room began to turn back toward Aria. "Let me see you do a pas de chat."

Aria stared. She had no idea what that was. "Um."

Miss Annette put her hands on her hips. "Fine. A plié."

Mikayla had slipped into the room. Aria could see her standing behind the instructor. At the word *plié*, Mikayla brought her hands up in front of her, like she was holding a basket, and dipped down, her legs bowing. Aria did her best to mimic this. Miss Annette made an exasperated sound.

"A grand jeté."

At that, Aria smiled. She knew how to do that one: the jump! She took a few steps back, then managed her best running leap. She was quite proud of herself, but Miss Annette only clicked her tongue.

"Do you at least have a routine you can show me?"

"Right here?" asked Aria. "Right now?"

"You are standing in a dance studio, and yes, now."

Aria swallowed. She wasn't self-conscious — she was a terrible singer and had still belted out tunes to help Gabby Torres — but this was different. Aria didn't usually care about looking silly or stupid, but here, she knew that if she wasn't good enough, they'd kick her out, and if that happened, it would be a lot harder to help Mikayla. She looked down at her shadow, but she knew it couldn't help her, not with this.

"Well?" pressed Miss Annette.

Aria nodded. "All right."

"Do you have music?" Miss Annette asked, pointing to the iPod speakers at the front of the room.

"Oh," said Aria. "No. Any song will do."

Miss Annette looked skeptical, but crossed to the iPod. A dozen dancers had now appeared in the studio to watch her, but it was Mikayla's gaze Aria could feel as she closed her eyes and took a breath. The music started. It was a pop song, one of the ones she'd sung with Gabby back in her room. Weeks ago. Lifetimes ago. Aria listened to it for a few moments, bouncing on her toes, finding the beat.

And then, as smoothly as she could, she started moving her arms and legs. There was something about the music, something cheerful, and as she danced, she thought of the gardens in Brooklyn. She thought of trampolines, of sleepovers and swimming pools. She thought of cupcakes and fall leaves and singing with Gabby. She thought of things that made her happy. Things that made her feel alive. Real. Human. She let that feeling move her, literally.

And then, all of a sudden, the music stopped. Aria blinked, and looked up to see Miss Annette watching her, eyes narrowed in thought.

Aria didn't know what to do. She wasn't sure what came next.

The room was painfully quiet, and Aria glanced at Mikayla, hoping to find an encouraging smile. But to her surprise, the other girl didn't look happy at all. If anything, she looked sad and lost. Aria didn't understand.

What had she done to make her upset?

chapter 9

MIKAYLA

Mikayla stood against the wall with the other girls and watched Aria dance.

It had taken Aria a few moments to find the beat, to sink into the music. But then she was gliding across the floor. It wasn't perfect, far from it, but there was something to the movement, a kind of reckless abandon Mikayla envied. And *missed*.

Because back when Mikayla first started dancing, back before she cared about nailing every step, before she'd been afraid of making a mistake (before she'd even known what the mistakes *were*), she had moved like that, like Aria. The music would start, and she would just fall into it. Disappear.

She'd stop being Mikayla Stevens and become a melody, a rhythm, a beat. She'd stop thinking about the steps. She'd lose herself, and when that happened, she could be anyone, anything, for the length of the dance. It was the best feeling in the whole wide world.

Or at least, it used to be.

These days, the doubt and the fear and the pressure followed Mikayla wherever she went, and whenever she danced. Once in a while, when the music was perfect and nothing ached, the voices in her would quiet, and she'd start to lose herself again, just for a second. She'd forget how much it mattered, to her and to Miss Annette and to her parents. But those moments never lasted.

Now, Aria . . . Aria had danced like it didn't matter.

Like she didn't care if someone was watching.

Didn't care if she was messing up, or if she was good enough.

She just . . . danced.

"You're a beginner," Miss Annette said at last. It wasn't a question.

"I am." Aria nodded. "But," she added, "everyone has to start somewhere."

"Your form is a mess," added Miss Annette. "Your lines are far from straight and your hands need work, and it was, on the whole, a fairly rudimentary routine."

Aria kept her head up, but her smile flickered, and her gaze drifted not to the floor, but to the wall where Mikayla was standing.

"*But*," continued Miss Annette. "You have some natural talent. You dance with your heart. It's not enough, of course, but it's a start. I can teach you to dance with the rest."

"So I can stay?" asked Aria softly.

Miss Annette crossed her arms. "For now."

At that, Aria smiled like she'd just won Nationals.

As Mikayla returned to her Advanced studio and went through her arabesques and pirouettes, her tumbles and turns, she couldn't stop thinking of Aria's smile. Or the look on her face when she was dancing, lost in the music.

The girls at Filigree always looked focused, or tired, stressed or aching or worried or determined.

But Aria just looked *happy*.

The sun was going down by the time dance class ended. Mikayla and Sara and Aria all pulled on their jackets and descended the steps to the street. Sara peeled away — she lived on the Upper West Side and could walk home — and Mikayla and Aria made their way to the subway together.

"You're awfully quiet," said Aria as they walked.

"Just thinking," said Mikayla. "And tired."

Aria yawned. "I know," she said. "I can't believe you do this six days a week."

Mikayla shrugged. She tried not to focus on that, because it was a slippery slope from tired to whiny, and Miss Annette had a zero-tolerance policy when it came to complaints. Of course Mikayla was tired — exhausted in a bone-deep way — but she'd gotten over it, or at least gotten used to it. It was just another sacrifice.

Success requires sacrifice. One of Miss Annette's many sayings.

When the train came and they got on, Mikayla snagged two seats. Aria slumped down beside her. "How do you do it all?" she asked, sounding genuinely amazed.

Mikayla shrugged again. She didn't just do it for herself. She did it for her parents, who had sacrificed so much for so long to make it possible. The Drexton audition loomed in the back of her mind. She was so close. If she could just get in, she'd finally be able to make it up to them.

Aria stretched, obviously sore after the long lesson. The subway train sped through several stops. It was an express.

Mikayla hesitated, then said, "Why did you decide to come to Filigree today?"

Aria's forehead crinkled. "What do you mean?"

"I mean, I know you hadn't been accepted yet. Which means you just . . . decided to come."

Aria tugged her red hair out of its bun and shrugged. "Maybe I was inspired by you. Maybe I just felt drawn to it. Like fate."

Mikayla sighed. "It's not fate if you *make* paths cross, Aria."

Aria gave a half-smile. "Even though I nudged our paths a little," she said, "I still think we were supposed to meet."

And it was weird; Mikayla couldn't explain why, but she felt the same way. "I'm glad we did," she said. "It was pretty bold of you to just dance like that, in front of everyone."

"Oh man," said Aria with a chuckle. "It was pretty bad, wasn't it?"

"No," said Mikayla. "I mean, okay, technically there were issues, but that's just because you're new."

Aria sighed. "There's *so* much I don't know."

"I could help you learn." It wasn't an *entirely* selfless offer. Some small part of Mikayla hoped that maybe by being near Aria, she could rediscover the way dance used to feel, even though all afternoon it had been a reminder of something she'd lost.

Aria laughed and sat forward. "I'm supposed to be the one helping you."

Mikayla frowned. "What do you mean?"

Aria's eyes widened, as if she'd surprised herself. "Nothing," she said, blushing. "Sorry, my brain must be tired. And thanks. That would be great."

The subway train shuddered to a stop, and the doors dinged open. People pushed on and off, and then the doors closed. Mikayla was glad they'd gotten seats.

"I'll do what I can to help," she told Aria. "My form's not perfect."

"You're *way* too hard on yourself," said Aria. "You're an incredible dancer. And *perfect* is kind of a silly word."

"How so?" Mikayla bristled a little.

"Well," said Aria. "There's no such thing as perfect. It doesn't exist."

"Of course it does."

"Where?" challenged Aria. "If perfect means without flaws, then there's no such thing as a perfect tree, or a perfect apple, or a perfect sky."

"What about a perfect score?" asked Mikayla. "That exists."

"Even if *you* got a perfect score," said Aria with a devious smile, "I bet you'd find mistakes."

Mikayla found herself blushing. She didn't know how Aria knew that, but she was right.

"Perfect is this thing in your head," continued Aria. "If you think, *I'll be happy when I'm perfect*, then you'll never be happy! I just don't think perfect is a good thing to shoot for."

"Well," said Mikayla. "You still have to try."

"Why?" asked Aria, sounding genuinely curious.

"Because," said Mikayla with exasperation, "even if there's no such thing as *perfect*, there *is* such a thing as *best*. And in the world of dance, being the best is what matters. It's *all* that matters."

The smile slid from Aria's face, and Mikayla felt bad for saying those words so harshly. But it was true. Aria could let go, dance like she didn't care, but for Mikayla, it wasn't about having fun, not anymore.

It was about *winning*.

A silence fell between them as the train rattled toward Brooklyn.

"This is my stop," Mikayla said when the train screeched to a halt in her station. "I'll see you tomorrow, okay?" She wondered where Aria lived, but she wouldn't have time to stop and ask if she wanted to make it off the train.

"Sure thing," said Aria, summoning a smile. Mikayla got off, but when she looked back, just before the train pulled away, she was surprised to see the smile slide from Aria's face, replaced by worry.

Mikayla pulled her jacket tight around her and hurried home. When she reached the front steps, she hesitated, dragged down by the thought of her father hunched at the kitchen table, the boxes looming in the corners, the gold trophies lining the basement walls. A lump filled her throat.

She brought her forehead to the front door.

Here's what will happen, she told herself. *Next week, I'm going to nail my audition at Drexton. I'm going to get the scholarship, and Mom and Dad won't have to pay for dance or Coleridge anymore, and Dad will get a new job, and we won't lose our house, and everything will be perfect. Because I will be perfect.*

And then she took a deep breath, readjusted her smile, and went in.

chăpter 10

ARIA

Aria didn't get off the train.

She'd thought about following Mikayla, but instead she hung back and watched the girl go, tendrils of blue trailing in her wake.

Aria needed to think, and something about the motion of the train, as it made its winding path, was soothing. A map on the wall showed the whole city — it looked so small and so large at the same time — and all the train lines criss-crossing over the top of it, labeled things like A and B and 1 and 2 and 3. They were all different colors, too.

Aria ran a thumb absently over the bare ring on her charm bracelet, trying to sort through the mystery of Mikayla Stevens. Back in California, Caroline's problem had been fairly obvious, and, at least in retrospect, Gabby's had been clear, too. But Aria was having trouble understanding Mikayla.

As the train clattered along, Aria thought about all the things Mikayla had said — about money, the need to be the best, the way her life revolved around dance — and all the things she hadn't. She thought of the boxes at Mikayla's house, but also the weary sadness that wove through her voice when she spoke of dancing.

Aria thought about Mikayla as a dancer. After Aria had performed for Miss Annette, she'd made herself invisible and watched through a crack in the door as Mikayla danced in the Advanced studio. Mikayla had seemed fidgety. She was constantly adjusting her posture, holding in her stomach, forcing a smile she obviously didn't feel. Like she wasn't comfortable in her own skin. Aria had seen the self-criticism swirling in her smoke.

But then . . . there were those moments, embedded in the middle of a routine, when it was like all that fell away, and she seemed genuinely happy to be dancing. And in those moments, the smoke around her changed, too. Didn't lessen or thin, exactly, but shifted. *Reacted*.

So did that make dance the *problem*, or the *solution*?

Or could it somehow be both at once?

Aria looked down at her shadow, as if it had something to say. But it didn't, so Aria leaned back. She stayed on the subway, riding it from end to end, changing from the blue line to the red to the green, trading As and Cs for 1s and 2s and Gs.

As it got later, she started to stand out more and more (apparently twelve-year-old girls didn't ride the subway alone after a certain time), and finally, between stops, when no one was there to see, Aria took a breath and willed herself to disappear.

She didn't like being invisible, but it definitely made things easier sometimes.

As evening turned to night, the crowd on the subway thinned. There was a man with a bike. A tired-looking woman with grocery bags. A figure stretched out sleeping across three seats. And that's how Aria realized, with some surprise, that she wasn't the only one without a place to call home.

At different stations, Aria began to see these people: slumped or dozing on the benches, looking lost and tired and ragged. None of them were surrounded by blue smoke. None of them were marked for Aria's help. But that didn't mean she couldn't try and make their lives a little better. She put coins in cups, mended coats and blankets and shoes with an invisible touch. Even if the acts of kindness were small, and wouldn't bring her any closer to helping Mikayla and earning her wings, they still made her feel useful.

After she'd ridden a few more trains, Aria decided to get some fresh air.

When she got up to the street, she was amazed to find that the sparkling city was still very much awake. It felt even bigger at night, and Aria felt even smaller. But it wasn't a bad kind of small. It made her feel like a piece of something. Connected. She wandered down the sidewalk, past dimly lit restaurants and brightly lit markets, and businesses closed for the night.

She passed a handful of chalk murals on the sidewalk, stepping gingerly around them so she wouldn't mess them up. They were so beautiful and colorful and intricate that it took her several moments to realize they were words. Sayings like *This Too Shall Pass* and *Take a Deep Breath, It Will All Be Okay* and *Find Your Joy.*

Clever sidewalk, she thought.

A streetlamp behind her cast her shadow forward so that it almost looked like it was part of the picture, the words of encouragement bubbling around its head.

A bucket of chalk sat nearby, with a small sign that said, ADD YOUR VOICE.

Aria wondered what she should write, and was still wondering when she heard the sound of laughter. She followed it, and found a group of teenage boys passing a basketball back and forth, taking leisurely shots at a net. Farther down the block, a movie theater was spilling out a group of girls, arms linked. Across the street, a cupcake shop was jam-packed with laughing customers.

All these people had something in common.

They all looked like they were having *fun*.

Maybe *that* was what Mikayla was missing. Aria thought back, and realized that even though they'd spent most of the day together, she'd never once heard Mikayla laugh. Not even with her friends at lunch. She had that smile, but it faltered when no one was looking. And even though she had perfect posture, she seemed to be bending under the weight of her life. The pressure. The expectation. The responsibility.

Maybe that was it. Maybe Mikayla was taking on too much.

After all, she was only twelve.

When was the last time she'd acted like it? Maybe Mikayla Stevens needed to shrug off that weight, and have a little fun. It couldn't hurt.

Aria retraced her steps toward the mural.

She smiled, and took up a piece of blue chalk and added her own message to the edge of the swirling letters. Two small words.

Have Fun.

chapter 11

MIKAYLA

"Stop, stop, stop," snapped Miss Annette in dance class the next afternoon.

In the midst of spinning, Mikayla lost her balance and staggered.

"Where's your head?" challenged her coach. "Because it's not here."

Miss Annette was right.

Mikayla hadn't slept. She couldn't stop thinking about what Aria had said on the subway, about there being no such thing as perfect. In fact, ever since the strange redheaded girl had showed up in Mikayla's life, her words had been burrowing into Mikayla's thoughts, snagging there like thorns.

You're way *too hard on yourself.*
You're an incredible dancer.

There's no such thing as perfect.

Mikayla had lain there in her bed, looking at the poster across the room.

WINNERS NEVER QUIT. QUITTERS NEVER WIN.

Downstairs, she'd heard her parents talking. About her. About money. About dance.

We'll find a way . . .

She's worked so hard . . . we have to . . .

"I'm sorry," said Mikayla to Miss Annette now, trying to shake the questions and the voices of out of her limbs.

"I don't want sorry," snapped Miss Annette. Mikayla cringed. Miss Annette often seesawed between treating her like a star and being harder on her than she was on anyone else. Mikayla guessed the two were connected — Miss Annette insisted she was tough on Mikayla because she believed in her, believed she was made of gold, but it didn't feel that way. "Just do it again," Miss Annette added sharply. "And do it right."

Mikayla took a deep breath and started the turn again. She focused, agonized over every motion, so intent that she didn't even feel the dancing, didn't hear the music, only the marks she was supposed to hit. By the time Mikayla came to a stop, she felt strangely hollow and sad, but she'd made it through without another mistake.

"That's more like it," said Miss Annette. "Ten minute break!" she called out to the rest of the room, clapping her hands.

Mikayla escaped before Miss Annette could decide to make her stay and go again.

Aria's class was also on their break and Mikayla saw Aria in the common hallway, putting on her sneakers. She and Aria hadn't interacted much at school that day, but Mikayla had been pleasantly surprised when Aria had again walked along with her and Sara over to Filigree. Something about Aria's presence made Mikayla feel lighter. Even scowling Sara didn't seem quite so bad when Aria was around.

"Come on," Aria said now, hopping to her feet.

"Where are we going?" asked Mikayla, wiping the sweat off her brow.

Aria nodded at the window, toward the small park behind Filigree's building. "Outside."

Mikayla shook her head. "We only have ten minutes." During the class breaks, the girls would stretch in the common hallway, or use the restroom, or work on nailing their turns. True, there was no explicit rule that they couldn't step into the park. . . .

Aria smiled. "You can do a lot in ten minutes," she said. "And it's gorgeous out, not cold at all. Didn't you notice on the way here?" Mikayla hadn't. "Besides," added Aria, "you look like you could use some fresh air."

Mikayla suddenly realized that fresh air was *exactly* what she needed. A few moments of freedom from Filigree. So she ducked into the changing room and slipped on her own shoes, adding her jacket as well. When the other girls stretching in the hall noticed that Aria and Mikayla were heading out, they glanced over with something like envy.

"Everyone here looks like they could use a little air," Aria observed, glancing around. "And maybe a little *fun*. When's the last time you had some?"

Mikayla rolled her eyes, even though the truth was, she couldn't remember.

Clearly intrigued, a few of the other girls took Aria up on her offer. Donning shoes and jackets, they trailed outside. Even Sara, who looked skeptical, came along. Aria led the way, and Mikayla walked beside her, feeling at once guilty and excited to be stepping out of the building for a bit.

The park was a small stretch of green fenced off and dotted with trees. Mikayla looked up at the streaks of cloud and the bright blue sky. It really *was* a pretty afternoon. She wondered how Beth and Katie were spending it, if Alex was out on his bike. She wondered how *she'd* spend the afternoon, if she weren't here. Which was a stupid thing to wonder, so she forced herself to stop.

The girls gathered in a loose circle, eyeing Aria uncertainly.

"Well?" asked one of the dancers from Mikayla's class, Elin.

"What are we doing out here?" asked another advanced dancer named Nissa.

Aria tapped her shoe and chewed her lip. "Why don't we play a game?" she offered.

Sara groaned. "Games are for little kids," she complained, just as Nissa asked, "What kind of game?"

At that, Aria smiled, reached out, and touched Sara's shoulder.

"Tag," she said. "You're it."

At first, nobody moved. Mikalya wanted to say that they needed to conserve their energy for class, that she was still sweaty from her turns. The other girls seemed to feel the same way, standing and waiting for someone to do something.

And then, it just kind of *happened*.

Sara took a single step forward, and on instinct, everyone else jumped back.

She took another step, and everyone took off running, including Mikayla.

It felt nice to run, to move her body without worrying about tempo and getting the steps right. The girls ran in every direction, and in seconds the park was filled with the sounds of laughter. Sara went after Nissa. Mikayla's heart raced as she ducked behind a tree. Aria lunged behind the one beside her.

Sara skimmed Nissa's arm, and they reversed direction, Sara fleeing as Nissa took off after Elin, who then took off after Aria and Mikayla. Aria ran ahead, her red curls flying, but she was tagged next. Aria and Mikayla exchanged a look — Mikayla could feel herself smiling — and then Aria took off after her, and Mikayla ran, the two sprinting across the grass.

For a few, glorious strides, Mikayla felt *happy*. Like the weight of the world — her parents, the boxes, school, Miss Annette, the Drexton audition — just fell away and she could breathe.

She didn't notice the root sticking out of the grass, not until it caught her shoe and sent her sprawling forward hard. A sharp pain shot up her ankle. She gasped, more from the shock of the fall than the pain. Then she tried to stand, and this time the gasp was a mix of pain and panic, because something was very, very wrong with her foot.

The girls immediately rushed around her.

"Mikayla?"

"Can you stand?"

"What happened?"

"Stay still."

And then Aria was there, crouching next to her. Her blue eyes were full of regret. "I'm so sorry," she said. "It wasn't supposed to go this way. I just wanted to —"

But she didn't get a chance to finish. Miss Annette had burst through the back doors and was hurrying across the park. She shoved the girls out of the way.

"Everyone get back! What are you doing outside during break? What on earth has happened here?"

"We were just —" started Aria again, but then Miss Annette saw Mikayla on the ground, holding her ankle, and she let out a sound of dismay.

Miss Annette crouched beside her and prodded Mikayla's sore ankle. Mikayla bit her lip to keep from crying out.

Mikayla saw that Aria was still watching her worriedly. It was the strangest thing, but the shadow at Aria's feet seemed to waver. Mikayla decided she had imagined it, that she was delirious from the pain.

"Is she okay? Can you help her stand up?" Elin asked worriedly.

Miss Annette's face became a rigid mask of concern and anger, but for once she was silent as she scooped Mikayla into her arms, and stormed away.

chāpter 12

ARIA

Aria saw it all happen a second too late.

If she had seen it just in time, her shadow might have come to life and carried her over to catch Mikayla before she fell. But it had all happened too fast, and now Aria sat cross-legged on a very uncomfortable bench in a hospital hall, feeling horrible and helpless and totally responsible. She was just trying to help — she was always trying to help — but she'd somehow made things worse.

She looked down at her bracelet and wondered if an angel could *lose* feathers for messing up.

Mikayla was in with the doctors and Miss Annette, getting her ankle examined. Her mom was on her way. Aria hadn't been in a hospital since her time with Gabby. Those had been different circumstances, of course, and a different hospital altogether. But the pale halls still felt sadly familiar.

Aria fiddled with the empty loop on her charm bracelet, feeling like she had her own cloud of smoke hanging around her shoulders. It wasn't that Aria thought a game of tag would suddenly solve all of Mikayla's problems. But she hoped it would get Mikayla out of her head and show her that not everything was win or lose. Some things were just for fun. It certainly couldn't hurt.

Only, it had.

Miss Annette stomped out of Mikayla's exam room, flustered, and turned her attention on Aria. She didn't ask what Aria was doing there, or even how she'd gotten there. (Miss Annette had driven Mikayla to the hospital herself.) Instead, she knelt down and glowered in Aria's face.

"What were you thinking?" she growled.

"We were just playing a game," said Aria. "I didn't think —"

"No, you didn't think. You just gambled with my best dancer. She could have broken her ankle! And with Drexton coming up." Miss Annette shook her head, as if she couldn't bear to think about it. "As it is, she'll be off for days. DAYS."

Aria was glad to hear that Mikayla's ankle wasn't broken, and thought *days* didn't seem like long at all, especially if it meant she'd be okay. But Miss Annette acted like it was the end of the world. "I've changed my mind about you," the teacher went on ferociously. "You're no longer welcome at Filigree."

Aria's heart sank. "But I —"

Before Aria could say anything else, Miss Annette straightened up and stormed off down the hall, muttering to herself, "I don't have time for this. . . ."

Aria watched, glad when she was gone.

Then she stood and glared down at her shadow. "You could have helped me," she said, even though she knew it wasn't the shadow's fault. Or maybe it was. But for all her talk about fate, she had a hard time believing this was how things were supposed to happen.

Aria sighed and knocked on Mikayla's door. A moment later she heard a quiet voice say, "Come in."

Mikayla looked up from where she lay on the exam table. She'd obviously been expecting a doctor and was surprised to see an Aria instead. Surprised, but not angry.

"Aria," she said. "What are you doing here?"

"I was worried," answered Aria. "The game was my idea, and I had no idea this would happen. I'm so sorry. . . ."

"Don't be," said Mikayla, shaking her head. "It's not your fault. You couldn't have done anything to stop it."

Could I? Aria wondered, sinking into a nearby chair. *I'm your guardian angel.* Somehow the fact that Mikayla didn't seem mad at her made Aria feel even worse.

Mikayla's ankle was wrapped and propped up on several pillows.

"How bad is it?" Aria asked, wishing not for the first time that she was a different kind of angel, one who could actually *fix* broken things.

"It's just twisted," said Mikayla.

"That must be a relief," said Aria.

"Yeah," mumbled Mikayla. But Aria was surprised to see a shadow cross the girl's face, and her blue smoke darken and coil around her.

"I'm sorry," said Aria, feeling like if she said it any more times, it would start to lose its meaning.

Mikayla sank back against the exam table. "The doctor said I'm supposed to stay off of it," she said. "Just for a few days. So no dancing." She tipped her head back. Her smoke swirled. "Do you really believe that everything happens for a reason?"

Aria hesitated, then found herself nodding. "Why?"

"It's just . . . I don't know . . . lately I've been wondering what my life would be like if I weren't spending every single moment dancing. And then . . ." she gestured to her ankle. "This happened."

Aria looked down at her shadow, thinking. She *did* believe things happened for a reason. Or at least, that everything had the potential to matter. Now she wondered if somehow this, the fall, the twisted ankle, was supposed to happen because Mikayla needed a break. A chance to step away from dance. To see that a person was made up of more than one thing. This was her chance. Maybe it would help.

Or maybe Aria was just trying to make herself feel better.

"It *was* fun," Mikayla spoke up, and Aria looked at her, surprised but glad. "At least for a little while." Mikayla almost smiled. Aria started to smile, too. Silence fell over them like a blanket. Then Mikayla said, "Can I tell you something?"

"Of course," said Aria.

"You promise not to judge me?"

"I don't judge anyone," said Aria. "I'm just here to help."

Mikayla considered her ankle, while Aria considered the girl's blue smoke. "When I fell," she said at last, "the first thing I felt, after pain, wasn't fear or sadness. It was *relief.* I was *relieved* at the thought of not having to go back into Filigree. Of having an excuse to not dance."

And there it was. The heart of Mikayla's problem, the reason Aria was there.

Mikayla looked up, her eyes wide. "Isn't that awful?"

"No," answered Aria. "It's just honest."

Mikayla sighed.

Aria took a deep breath. "I think that sometimes people have a really hard time being honest with themselves."

Mikayla's stress and conflicting thoughts were all tangled up in her smoke. She had probably been feeling these things for a long time, and simply hadn't stopped to look at them. Hadn't wanted to.

"Sometimes," Aria went on, "something has to happen to make someone face what's wrong in their life."

"But dance *is* my life."

"Do you love it?" asked Aria.

Mikayla opened her mouth. Closed it. Opened it again. "I . . . I did." She put her head in her hands. "I mean I do. I don't know, Aria."

"It's okay."

"No it's not. This is my life. It's who I am."

Aria wanted to say that people were more than what they

did, but then the door burst open and Mikayla's mom was there, a whirlwind of worry and nervous energy, of *oh no* and *how are you feeling* and *I came as soon as I heard* . . .

And Aria knew that this wasn't the time or the place, so she stepped back, and slipped out the door.

chapter 13

MIKAYLA

Mikayla's mom let her stay home from school the next day.

It was a Friday, and Mikayla's first thought was that she couldn't miss dance, before she remembered that she couldn't *go*. It took her by surprise again, the wave of relief that came before the dread.

The Drexton audition was only a week away, and she knew she needed the practice. But for the next few days, dance was off-limits.

But without dance, and without school to distract her from its absence, she felt lost.

What did people actually *do* with their free time?

It was a drizzling gray day; her mom had stayed home from work and was bustling around the house — as far as Mikayla could tell, she was putting things in boxes — and her dad was at another interview. Chow was asleep at her feet. Mikayla was propped up on the couch with her ankle wrapped in ice.

Both Beth and Katie had texted to check on her, and Katie even asked if she should come over after school. But Mikayla had looked around at the moving boxes and said no, she was fine.

And now, for the first time in forever, she almost felt *bored*.

It was such a strange thing, sitting still. She tried to do homework, but her thoughts kept wandering. She flipped through the channels, but nothing held her interest. Finally she put her earbuds in and cranked the music up, even though it made her want to get up and move, and she couldn't.

And then — she wasn't sure how much time had passed, how many songs had gone by — someone tapped her shoulder, and she jumped, sending a tiny wave of pain through her foot. She tugged the earbuds out and twisted to find Aria standing in her living room.

Chow hadn't heard her come in either, and now he sprang to his feet, barking. But when Aria reached out and started petting him, he promptly flopped over at her feet.

Which was surprising. Chow wasn't usually that friendly to strangers.

"Sorry," said Aria. "Didn't mean to frighten you. Your mom let me in."

"What are you doing here?" asked Mikayla. She checked the clock on the wall. It wasn't even noon. "Shouldn't you be at school?"

Aria smiled, and readjusted the backpack on her shoulder. "I thought you could use some company," she said, adding, "I don't think they'll miss me."

"Are you going to Filigree later?" asked Mikayla. "Miss Annette has a really strict no-skipping policy."

"Yeah, about that . . ." said Aria slowly, "I kind of had my acceptance revoked." Mikayla felt her eyes widen. "But it's okay!" added Aria quickly. "Filigree and I weren't a good fit."

Mikayla stared at the other girl. She couldn't make sense of Aria Blue. This girl who had just walked into her life and turned it upside down. But she was glad Aria was there.

"So do you have any siblings?" asked Aria, looking around. "Are they dancers, too?"

"No," said Mikayla. "I'm an only child. You?"

"Same," said Aria. "It's just me."

Mikayla fell silent a moment, and then she said, "I some-times wish I had siblings."

"For the company?" asked Aria.

"No," said Mikayla. "Not really."

"Then what?" Aria put a hand on Mikayla's shoulder, and Mikayla could feel the words about to spill out.

She looked down. "For the pressure," she said. "When you're an only child, all eyes are on you. You're always the one responsible . . . Sometimes I think it would be nice if my parents had someone else to focus on. Then I wouldn't feel like everything was riding on me." Aria's hand slipped away, and Mikayla blinked. She hadn't meant to open up like that, and she shook her head. "I shouldn't complain," she scolded herself. "Honestly."

"I think it makes sense," said Aria. And then, to Mikayla's relief, she changed the subject. "So," she said cheerfully. "No dance. No school. What will you do with all your time?"

"I have no idea," said Mikayla.

"Sure you do."

Mikayla shook her head. "You asked me the other day, what I do when I'm not dancing, and I didn't answer because I couldn't think of anything. Because I'm never not dancing."

"You're not dancing right now," observed Aria casually.

"Right, and I'm *bored stiff*," Mikayla shot back. "I don't even know what to do."

"Cut yourself some slack," said Aria with a laugh. "I bet it's hard to think of things to do when you're confined to a couch."

Aria started digging through her backpack. And then she pulled out a notepad and a pen, and perched on the arm of the couch.

Mikayla shook her head. "It's more than that," she said, lowering her voice. "Dance is not just what I *do*. It's who I *am*. So I don't know how to be me without it." It scared her to admit that.

Aria rapped the pen against the pad a few times, thinking. "Okay, so dance is your life," she said. "It defines you." Mikayla nodded. "But it's a thing," Aria went on. "You're not a thing, you're a *who*. A person. And people are more than one thing. They're messy, in the best way. They're made up of everything they've done, everyone they've been, and everyone they'll be. Even though you're an amazing dancer, it's not *all* you are."

Mikayla's heart sank. She wanted to believe that, but she didn't see how it was true. She nodded at the pen and paper. "What's that for?"

Aria brightened. "We're going to make a list," she said. "Together. And then, when you're feeling better, you can do the things on it. So," she held the pen out between them, as if it were a microphone, "if you had all the time in the world, what would you do?"

Mikayla opened her mouth to protest, because she'd never have all the time in the world, and even if she did, she probably couldn't afford to do half the things she wanted. But then she stopped. There was something about Aria's expression, the simple, unguarded hope, that made her play along.

"I'd go to the movies," Mikayla answered. "I'd see everything that's playing in the theater."

Aria scribbled this down.

"And I'd ride my bike through Prospect Park with Alex."

"He says hi, by the way," cut in Aria. "I met him the other day." Mikayla's chest tightened. "Okay, what else?"

"I'd . . ." Mikayla bit her lip. "I'd bake cookies. I'd reread all the Harry Potter books. I'd get frozen hot chocolate at Serendipity with Beth and Katie. I'd play tennis with Beth and draw with Katie, and I'd walk along the High Line, and go the Met museum, and sleep in and . . ." she trailed off, breathless, her head rushing from all these possible activities, and feeling guilty that none of them were dance.

Aria finished writing and turned the list toward Mikayla with a smile. "I think that's a good start. So . . ." She tore the page free of the notepad and held it out to Mikayla. "What should we do first?"

chapter 14

ARIA

"Wait!" said Mikayla. "I think you're supposed to *measure* the ingredients before you put them in."

"It's more fun when you guess," said Aria, scooping sugar into the mixing bowl.

They were standing in the kitchen — well, Aria was standing, Mikayla was sitting on a stool — making cookies, because that was one of the only things on the list that didn't require the ability to walk. Chow circled their legs, lapping up anything that fell.

"Girls," called Mikayla's mom from the living room. "Try not to make a mess."

Aria looked at Mikayla, who was covered in flour, and Mikayla looked at Aria, who was covered in sugar, and the two burst into laughter.

Aria didn't realize how old Mikayla had looked before, until she started laughing and looked much younger. Her smoke thinned a little. Aria knew it wasn't enough, that it was a shallow kind of happy, but it was still nice to see her laugh.

"So . . ." said Aria as they put the first batch of sugar cookies in the oven. "Are you guys moving?"

"What?" asked Mikayla, brushing flour from her T-shirt.

"The boxes," said Aria, looking around at the containers gathered in the corners of the room, the yet-to-be-assembled ones slouched in the hall.

"Oh," said Mikayla slowly. "I don't know. I guess it just depends." She looked down at her hands, and Aria could see the fears swirling in her smoke.

Aria reached out and touched the girl's arm, even though it left a sugary handprint there. "On what?"

Mikayla swallowed. "On whether my dad finds a new job soon. He's an engineer," she went on. "He used to work for this big product design firm. But it went under a few months ago, and he's been looking for a new position ever since. I wish I could do something. . . ."

"It's not your fault," said Aria softly. "And it's not your job —"

"I haven't told anyone about Dad," Mikayla went on, her cheeks flushing. "Not even Beth or Katie."

"Why not?" asked Aria.

"It's not like they can say or do anything to help, and . . ." she trailed off, obviously embarrassed, though Aria didn't see why she should be. "Beth and Katie are great," she added. "We've been friends forever, but they've never had to worry about money. I'm pretty sure they were given credit cards when they started kindergarten. I don't want them to get weird, to treat me like I don't belong."

"Do you honestly think they would?" asked Aria.

Mikayla dusted off her hands. "I don't know."

"Well, I'm glad you told *me*," said Aria, even though she didn't know how to help. She couldn't get Mikayla's dad a new job, couldn't save their house, any more than she could have cured Gabby's brother. She could only help Mikayla make the right choices when it came to her own path.

"I don't want to move," said Mikayla, so low Aria almost didn't hear. "I hate these boxes. I hate everything they mean."

"You know," said Aria after a moment, looking at the boxes again, "a house isn't really walls and a roof. It's the people inside, and you get to keep those no matter what. As far as these boxes, I think sometimes it's good to sort through our things, pack some away, pull others out. It reminds us who we've been, and who we are, and sometimes it helps us figure out who we want to be."

Just then, the timer dinged, and Aria hopped up to pull the cookies out of the oven. "These smell great!" she said, shuffling them onto a plate. "One item on Mikayla Stevens's Dance-Free To-Do List, done!"

Mikayla smiled, and found the flour-dusted list on the counter, and was just crossing off *bake cookies* when she heard the front door open, and close *hard*. She dropped the pen as her dad stormed in. He didn't even seem to see them as he slammed the briefcase down onto the table hard enough to make Chow jump. Then he sank into a chair.

"Dad?" whispered Mikayla as he put his head in his hands. He didn't seem to hear her, either.

Mikayla's mom appeared, took in the scene, and gave the girls a look that said it was time for Aria to go. Mikayla mouthed *I'm sorry* and Aria smiled and mouthed *don't be*, and then they managed a kind of *see you later* in a mix of nods and waves.

Aria slipped into the hall toward the front door. But she didn't leave. She opened the door, then closed it again, still standing in the foyer. She brought her hand to the wood,

93

watching as a moment later her hand disappeared, along with the rest of her.

Invisible Aria crept back to the kitchen doorway and saw Mikayla still sitting on the stool, her smoke swirling darker as she watched her mom try to comfort her dad. He loosened the tie at his throat and looked like he might cry. Aria watched Mikayla get down from the stool and use her crutches to hobble off toward her room. Aria didn't follow, not at first. She hung back, listening to the girl's parents.

"They've decided not to hire right now," said her dad, pulling the tie over his head.

"Don't give up," said her mom. "The Stevens aren't quitters."

"I don't know what to do. I'm running out of options."

"It'll be all right. We'll make it work. . . ."

He just kept shaking his head, and Aria wished that *he* was wreathed in smoke, marked for someone's help. Then she turned and followed Mikayla, slipping into her bedroom just before she closed the door.

Mikayla's room was so organized. No clothes on the floor. The bed was made and the desk was clear. The walls were covered in posters, and every single poster was about dance. Some showed girls leaping, or sitting elegantly on the floor; others were midturn, arms aloft. Aria turned and saw a poster on the back of Mikayla's door. A pair of dance shoes and a saying that made her frown.

WINNERS NEVER QUIT. QUITTERS NEVER WIN.

It seemed so . . . harsh. As Aria looked around, she realized that most of the posters had similar messages, about discipline, sacrifice, strength.

VICTORY IS WORTH THE PRICE.

NO PAIN, NO GAIN.

These were the words Mikayla read every morning and night? Aria shook her head. None of these sayings were about letting go, having fun, being happy. And dance was about that, too.

Aria watched, invisible, as Mikayla hit PLAY on her computer. Music filled the room, drowning out her parents' voices down the hall.

Aria sank onto the edge of the bed and watched as Mikayla tacked their to-do list up above her desk. Mikayla stared for a long time at the paper, and the question in her head and in her smoke was so loud, Aria could almost hear it.

Who would I be without dance?

Aria wanted to tell Mikayla there was only one way to find out, and that was to go looking for herself, for the person she'd been before, the one she wanted to be now. And then, as if Mikayla could hear her, her gaze drifted to the empty boxes. She hobbled to the edge of the bed and sat down facing her closet. Then she reached for the near-est box.

chapter 15

MIKAYLA

She knew she had to start, sooner or later. She might as well start now. Mikayla didn't have anything else to do — well, she could start rereading Harry Potter — but her mom had been nagging her for weeks to go through her closet.

You don't have to pack everything up, her mom had said. *Just go through, and see what you want to keep, and what you want to get rid of.*

Mikayla had been avoiding the chore as long as possible — she didn't have time, she was tired, she hoped that if she just ignored the boxes, they'd disappear . . . but they hadn't. And now, as she sat in front of the closet doors, she thought about what Aria had said. Not just about moving, but about finding who you are, who you want to be, and about the fact that people were made of more than one thing.

Mikayla couldn't remember a life outside of dance, but it had to be there, somewhere, buried.

She took a breath, leaned forward, and slid the closet doors open.

She pushed aside her school clothes and dance leotards and found a box of medals — silver and bronze, mostly. But behind that box, she found old dance costumes, as well as an album of pictures from her early days in dance. In these photos, Mikayla was nine, eight, seven, six, and beaming, even though she hadn't placed in half the competitions. Her costumes were strange and fanciful, the kind of thing Miss Annette would scoff at now. There were frills and gossamer, bright colors and ribbons and wings. Mikayla couldn't help but grin. They were fun. Whimsical.

Now Mikayla was taught, and reminded, to be her best self, her gold self. But looking at these things, she remembered a time when dancing had meant *transforming*, getting to be someone else. It had been an escape.

Dragging the costumes aside, Mikayla felt her way deeper into the closet, and came out with something else entirely.

A box of notebooks. The box itself was doodled and drawn on, with a ribbon tied around to hold it closed, as if it were precious.

Property of Mikayla Stevens, it said in a nine-year-old's handwriting.

She'd forgotten all about this. Inside she found a stack of notebooks, covered with drawings. Mikayla used to love drawing as much as dance. They both told stories. That was how she and Katie had first become friends, by bonding over drawing.

How had she forgotten about that?

As she flipped through the notebooks, she saw scribbles of story, along with doodles of dragons and fairies, ghosts and angels.

And the thing was, nine-year-old Mikayla had actually believed in them. Or at least, she'd wanted to. She'd been the kind of kid who wondered if her stuffed animals came to life when she was out of the room. The kind who left windows cracked for sprites and believed that old places were haunted. When her third-grade teacher had taken them to the American Museum of Natural History, and she'd seen the massive skeletons of dinosaurs, they'd made her believe in dragons. Because a world that could make such massive, incredible creatures could surely have made other monsters, too.

Mikayla had wanted to believe the world was full of things she couldn't see. Of higher powers, or at least *other* powers.

It seemed silly now. Childish. Mikayla Stevens had long since learned that the world wasn't full of magic and mystery, that there was no such thing as angels or ghosts or fate. *You* had to take responsibility for your own life, for your successes and your failures. That's what dance had taught her. What Miss Annette had taught her.

But sitting on the floor, surrounded by her childhood, Mikayla missed the girl who'd made these drawings, who'd worn these costumes and believed in magic. And she wondered, as she set the box of notebooks aside, if there was a way to get that Mikayla back, or if it was too late.

"It looks like a storm blew through here," said Aria the next day.

She was perched on Mikayla's bed, and the room was still covered in the contents of her closet. Mikayla had fallen asleep last night reading through one of her old notebooks, her costumes beneath her like a pillow.

When she'd woken up that Saturday morning, she'd avoided her parents, and it had been a welcome relief when Aria rang the doorbell, bright-eyed and holding fresh muffins from the local bakery.

"Sorry," Mikayla said now, massaging her still-sore ankle. "I decided to sort through some things last night."

"And what did you find?" asked Aria, biting into her muffin. "Mmm," she added, momentarily distracted. "This is kind of like a cupcake."

"Hang on," said Mikayla. She swiveled so that she and Aria were sitting side by side on the bed. Together, they flipped through the notebooks, and Mikayla tried to show Aria the person she'd been before dance, or at least before dance became so important, so big that it swallowed everything else.

Aria picked up a photo album and turned through it, pointing out photos of a goofy kid that Mikayla didn't even remember being. A kid who was eating a giant ice cream cone, making a mess and laughing. A kid who wore her dark curls in pigtails, big brown eyes shining as she stood outside the Central Park Zoo. If anything, the girl in the photos reminded Mikayla of *Aria*.

"When did things change?" asked Aria.

"I don't remember," said Mikayla, which was the truth. She felt like she should be able to pinpoint a day, a dance, a win — some moment when the gravity shifted and being the best became more important than having fun. But it must have happened over time, so slowly she didn't notice.

"I want to meet this girl," said Aria, tapping the album.

"I'm not her," said Mikayla. "Not anymore."

"Why not?"

"Because I was a kid. Monsters and magic, those are kids' ideas. I know better now."

"I still believe in magic," said Aria simply.

Mikayla rolled her eyes, even though Aria sounded completely serious. "Do you believe in monsters, too? Ghosts? Unicorns?" she asked teasingly.

Aria chewed her lip, as if thinking. "I believe the world is big and strange and full of wonder," she replied.

Mikayla was quiet. When Aria put it like that, it didn't sound quite as silly. Something in Mikayla's chest fluttered.

"What is Drexton?" asked Aria lightly, and the question jarred her. It sent a cold spike through her chest. Aria was pointing at the calendar on the wall, where the word was written in bold red letters. "I also heard Miss Annette mention it."

"Drexton Academy," said Mikayla. Aria looked at her blankly, so she explained. "It's the most prestigious dance school in the city. Probably in the *country*. They only take in a few new dancers each year — the auditions are invite-only — but if you get accepted, they pay for *everything*. Lessons.

Travel. Costumes. Competitions. Even a stipend for schooling."

"Wow."

"An audition window is coming up," continued Mikayla. "And I got an invitation to try out."

"That's amazing," said Aria.

"Yeah," said Mikayla, feeling nauseous.

"No matter what happens, you should be proud."

A heavy silence fell between them. Aria held out a muffin to Mikayla, and after a beat of hesitation, Mikayla accepted it and took a big bite. It had been ages since she'd let herself have something so sweet.

As she was eating the muffin, Aria glanced behind her, toward the shimmering pile of costumes on the bed. "Ohhh!" she said. "What are these?"

Mikayla let out a massive breath, relieved by the change of subject. "Old costumes," she said, swallowing, as Aria grabbed up a short iridescent dress. It seemed to change colors in her hands.

"I like this one," she said.

"Oh, that goes with these." Mikayla wiped her hands and reached past her into the closet. She pulled out a pair of iridescent wings. Aria's mouth fell open. "Here," said Mikayla. "Try them on."

Mikayla helped Aria drag the dress on over her clothes, and then she showed her how to slip her arms into the wings. When she was done, Aria turned to look at herself in the mirror on the wall. Her face broke into a huge grin, and Mikayla couldn't help but think that the wings suited her somehow.

Aria must have agreed, because she wore them the rest of the day.

Saturday went by in a blur of costume wings, old photo albums, and bad TV, books and drawings and laughter. Mikayla invited Aria to spend the night, and she happily stayed, sleeping on an air mattress on Mikayla's floor. Sunday was rainy, and the girls hid in Mikayla's room, reading random passages of Harry Potter inside a makeshift pillow fort (Aria was *really* good at making forts). Mikayla couldn't remember the last time she'd had so much fun. She almost forgot about her ankle, and Filigree, and the studio downstairs filled with trophies.

She might have succeeded, if Miss Annette hadn't called three times in those two days to check on her, and to remind her of the upcoming audition for Drexton.

Aria left Sunday night. By the time Mikayla got up for school on Monday, her ankle was stiff, the pain a dull ache. But she could walk more easily now, so there was no question it was getting better. Some small, guilty part of her wished that it wasn't healing so fast, even though the rest of her knew that it had to be better in time for the audition on Saturday. Her parents were still counting on her, and she couldn't let them down.

Her mom offered to drive her to the subway, but it was a gorgeous day, and she decided to walk and think through what to do with Aria after school. She was tying her laces gingerly on her front step when she heard a door open. She looked up to see Alex heading out.

He paused to adjust the chain on his bike. He'd gotten taller and his brown hair was longer and shaggier. How long had it been since she'd stopped and *really* looked at him? She felt her face grow warm.

"Hey, Alex," she said as she made her way down the steps, then leaned her elbows on the low chain fence between their houses.

He looked over and smiled. "Hey, stranger. How's dance?"

Mikayla glanced down. "It's fine," she lied, adding softly, "That's not *all* I do, you know."

"Could have fooled me," he said, teasingly.

"We should go ride our bikes in the park sometime," Mikayla said, looking back up at him and thinking of her list.

Alex smiled. "I'd like that," he said. "If you can find the time."

She blushed, but said, "I'll make time."

Alex swung his leg over his bike. "You want a lift to the subway?"

"Is that thing safe for two?"

Alex held out his hand. "Come on, M. Have a little faith."

chapter 16

ARIA

Aria sat on the school steps, working on her own list. She didn't want to tell Mikayla that she was making one, because it would be too complicated to explain.

But, sitting on the train the previous night, she'd conjured a piece of paper and pen and started writing. It wasn't much, just a list of places in the city she wanted to see, and things she wanted to do, before her time here was up.

Sometimes she cheated and added a place she'd already been — like the Botanic Garden — but she figured that was okay, since the list was just for her.

Go to a movie, she wrote.

Find the tallest building.

Visit Times Square.

"What's that?"

She glanced up to see Mikayla, looking well rested and happy, her dark hair loose instead of pulled back in its bun. Her smoke swirled around her, a little thinner, but still there.

"Just some notes," said Aria, getting to her feet. She was about to ask Mikayla how she was feeling, when Katie and Beth appeared, lavishing worry.

"M! How are you feeling?"

"Are you going to be okay?"

"Are you going crazy without dance?"

"I'm fine," said Mikayla, her smile shifting into the practiced one.

"How long are you off?" asked Sara snidely, who'd just appeared on the steps.

"Just a few days," said Mikayla, looking stiffer than ever.

"So you're still planning to audition at Drexton?" Sara pressed, narrowing her eyes.

Mikayla's smile flattened. "Of course," she said. Sara shrugged and went inside. The bell rang, and Mikayla and the others followed. Aria trailed after, watching the way Mikayla's smoke got darker every time she talked about dance.

Aria knew she needed to stop trying to *distract* Mikayla from her problems, and help her face them.

But she didn't know *how*. And she feared it wouldn't be easy.

"Park or museum?" asked Mikayla after school.

Without Filigree filling up her schedule, she'd taken it upon herself to show Aria around the city.

"Park," said Aria, looking at the sky. It was a beautiful day, a little cool, but sunny.

"We could do Prospect if we wanted to go back to Brooklyn now," Mikayla mused out loud. "But Central Park is much closer. Come on!"

They took the subway to Columbus Circle. Aria had ridden to that station before, invisibly at night, but she hadn't gotten off, had no idea what waited above. And nothing could prepare her, as they emerged, for the low stone gate that surrounded a massive, gorgeous sprawl of green.

"It's huge," she whispered to herself. Mikayla giggled. As they followed a path in, Aria stared around in awe at the trees and the rocks and the way the whole city just seemed to disappear, replaced by a forest, a lake, a hiking trail.

"Magical," Aria sighed, taking in a sloping green lawn that ended at a glittering pond.

Mikayla smiled. "Lots of people say that." She looked

around. "I guess I'd stopped seeing it. But you're right, it is." She smiled, a genuine, private smile. "I used to think Central Park was full of fairies, that they hid in the cracks of the big rocks, or in the lake. . . ."

Aria liked that idea. As Mikayla led her through the paths, Aria kept her eyes peeled for fairies. All around them, people were walking, jogging, laughing. Pushing strollers and walking dogs, eating ice cream and holding hands. Then, when Aria thought it couldn't get any better, she and Mikayla arrived at a zoo.

Aria had seen animals, of course. But she'd only been a person for a couple of months, so her experience had been limited to cats and dogs and birds and, since she'd arrived in New York, a few subway rats. Now, walking through the Central Park Zoo, Aria was *captivated*. She'd always thought that being an angel — or at least an angel-in-progress — was pretty cool, but the snow leopards, the penguins, and the monkeys seemed even cooler.

"You act like you've never seen a sea lion before," said Mikayla as Aria gaped at the incredible creature.

And the way she said it, like everyone — or at least everyone who had been someone for long enough — *had* seen them, made Aria say, "Not . . . like this. It's just so different when you're up close."

Aria held up her hand, and to her surprise — and everyone else's — one of the sea lions waddled toward her, as if eager to converse. *This*, thought Aria, for the fifteenth time that day, *is magical*. And then suddenly, as the sea lion wandered away, she felt a strange pang of sadness at the thought that the world was so big, so big that even if she had a thousand missions instead of three, she'd never get to see it all.

"What's wrong?" asked Mikayla.

Aria shook her head. "Nothing," she said, taking the girl's arm. "Where should we go next?"

"What do you want to see?" asked Mikayla.

Aria broke into a smile. "Everything."

Over the next few days, they went to the Museum of Natural History (where Aria could have stood staring at the dinosaur bones for hours), the Statue of Liberty (Aria loved the cool spray on her face from the ferry ride, and the grandeur of the statue on that tiny island), and Times Square (which was the strangest and brightest place Aria had *ever* seen; she was pretty sure there was more color and sound there than in the whole rest of the city, and Mikayla ended up having to lead her away).

Aria happily crossed items off her secret list just as Mikayla crossed items off hers. But as the week went on, and Mikayla's ankle got better, her smoke got worse, and she seemed more and more distracted. They'd avoided talking about dance, but Aria knew that avoiding a problem wasn't the same thing as overcoming it.

And it was time to talk.

It was Wednesday night, and they were sitting on her bed, reading from the Harry Potter books out loud and tossing out questions like, "Which house would you be sorted into?" (Aria felt she was strongly Hufflepuff, while Mikayla was certain they'd both be in Gryffindor) and "What would your Patronus look like?" But Mikayla kept glancing at the calendar on her bedroom wall.

"What's going on?" asked Aria at last.

Mikayla took one look at Aria, sighed, and said, "I'm going back to Filigree."

"When?"

"Tomorrow," she said. "My Drexton audition is on Saturday. I need to practice my routine."

"Are you ready?" asked Aria, and they both knew she wasn't asking about the strength of Mikayla's ankle.

Mikayla didn't answer that. Instead, she said, "I have to go back."

Aria chewed her lip. "Do you remember what you told me in the hospital? About being relieved?"

"Of course I do."

"Well," said Aria, slowly. "Don't you think there's a reason you felt that way? Something you should consider?"

"I was just tired," said Mikayla, sounding like she was trying to convince herself more than Aria. "I needed a break, but it's time to get back to work."

Aria reached out and touched her shoulder. "But if you don't love it anymore, then why —"

"Because I have to," she said.

"But do you *want* to?" asked Aria. Mikayla had been dancing for so long that people had stopped asking her if it was what she *wanted*. She had stopped asking herself. Nobody gave her the choice, because everyone assumed they knew the answer. But maybe someone needed to ask the question. The simple, important question.

"Mikayla," Aria said. "Do you want to quit dancing?"

chāpter 17

MIKAYLA

At first, all Mikayla heard was *quit*. She recoiled at the word.

"No," she said automatically. And then, "Of course not." And then, after a longer pause, "I *can't*."

"Of course you can," said Aria simply. It actually started to annoy Mikayla, the way Aria acted like it was such a small thing, to up and quit the biggest part of her life.

Mikayla shook her head, thinking of Miss Annette and Filigree and her parents and the wall of gold downstairs.

"You deserve to be happy," said Aria.

"Happy has nothing to do with it," snapped Mikayla.

"Shouldn't it?" countered Aria with a frown.

Mikayla shook her head. *Happy.* She struggled with that word. It was true, she'd felt happier these past few days than she had in ages. She certainly hadn't felt happy at the competition. Or in dance class.

It's just nerves, Miss Annette would say.

It's natural, her parents would insist.

This is the way it is, she'd tell herself.

After all, this was how it had been for as long as she could remember. No, that wasn't totally true. Mikayla thought of the girl in the photo album. Hadn't there been a time, in the beginning, when she danced because it made her happy? A time when she didn't dread getting on stage, didn't fear the failure of second place? What happened to that version of herself?

Mikayla shook her head again, as if she could clear the thoughts. Happy was simple, and this was complicated.

"I *miss* dancing," she insisted. And it wasn't a lie. She did. She didn't miss what it had *become*, but she missed what it used to be, when she first started, back before it all mattered *so* much. She hadn't missed Filigree, hadn't missed competing, hadn't missed feeling like no matter how hard she worked, it wasn't enough.

But she *wasn't* a quitter.

"The Drexton audition —" she started.

"Are you sure you want to do it?" challenged Aria.

"I have to," said Mikayla. "I don't expect you to understand."

"Then help me understand," pressed Aria.

Mikayla looked at her, long and hard. And then she stood up. "Okay," she said. "Follow me."

Mikayla flicked the switch in the basement, and the light glinted off the trophies. Mikayla hadn't been down here since her accident. She'd been avoiding the room, as if she could somehow avoid everything it represented. Out of sight, out of mind.

"Wow," said Aria quietly, taking in the wall of gold.

"The thing people don't understand," said Mikayla, running her fingers over a shelf of medals, "is that it's not enough to become the best. You have to *stay* the best. It's exhausting. People are always waiting for you to slip up, to go from gold to silver, to fail."

"Silver doesn't seem like failing."

Mikayla's fingers slid off the shelf. "It is when you're gold."

"All the gold's not worth it if you're miserable, Mikayla."

Mikayla's shoulders slumped. "You saw the boxes, Aria.

We don't have enough money. If dad doesn't get a new job soon, we're going to lose the house."

Aria eyed her thoughtfully. "But what does that have to do with Drexton?"

"Drexton would pay for dance, and school. It would help."

"So would quitting Filigree," observed Aria. She glanced up at the ceiling. "It's not your job to save this house, Mikayla. You can't take that on."

Mikayla's throat tightened. "My parents have given up so much, for so long. They've poured money into my classes. It's my job to make it worth it. It matters too much now. They need me to succeed. If I give up — if I *quit* — then it was all a waste. Every one of these gold trophies was for nothing. If I can just get through the audition . . ."

"Then what?" pressed Aria. "What happens when you get accepted?"

"If," corrected Mikayla.

"*If* you get in, Mikayla, then everything goes back to how it was, right? Only worse. You said Drexton was the most prestigious dance school in the city, right? So it's even *more* intense than Filigree. Are you sure you *want* to get in?"

Mikayla felt frustration bubbling inside her. "I've been working toward this for *years*, Aria. It's everything I've been training for. I can't just walk away."

Aria ran a hand through her curly red hair. "Why do you have to?" she asked. "Why does it have to be all or nothing? If what you miss is dancing, why can't you just . . . *dance*?"

Mikayla's chest tightened. "It's not that simple," she said.

"Why can't it be?"

"Because it's *not*," shouted Mikayla.

The words echoed through the small room.

"I'm sorry," said Mikayla, feeling bad for snapping at her friend.

"It's okay," said Aria. "I shouldn't have pushed you."

A moment later, Mikayla's mom appeared.

"Is everything okay?" she asked, looking worried.

Mikayla pulled her face into a forced smile. "We're fine," she said. "I was just telling Aria how excited I am to get back to dance tomorrow."

Her mom looked relieved. She crossed the room and kissed the top of Mikayla's head. "I'm proud of you," she said. "And I know you'll do wonderfully."

Mikayla found Aria's eyes in the mirrored wall, a crease of concern between them, but she turned away. "Thanks, Mom."

The next day, Mikayla went back to dance.

She said good-bye to Aria after school, part of her wishing they could go on another adventure. Like seeing paintings in a museum, or shopping in Union Square. But instead she followed Sara to Filigree, telling herself she just had to get through the Drexton audition.

Aria's question — *Then what?* — echoed in her head, but she pushed it away.

"What, no shadow?" asked Sara, obviously referring to Aria.

"She decided she didn't like Filigree," said Mikayla, not wanting to tell Sara that Miss Annette had kicked her out.

"Well," said Sara, smugly. "Quitters never win." The words Mikayla was so familiar with sounded meaner than usual, coming out of Sara's mouth. Or maybe they'd always been harsh.

As they climbed the stairs to the dance studio, Mikayla asked, "Did I miss anything?"

Sara shrugged, smirking. "I guess we'll find out."

Inside, Miss Annette wrapped Mikayla in a sequined embrace. "You gave us a scare," she said, pulling back. "Are you still my golden girl?"

Mikayla's chest tightened, and she felt herself slip back into her performance smile. "Absolutely."

Class started. Mikayla had only been gone for a few days, but she already felt like she'd fallen behind. Why hadn't she stretched more on her time off? She could have stayed limber, could have practiced her stance and her arms. Now her leaps weren't as high as they'd been, her lines weren't as perfect. She tried to stop the negative thoughts, tried not to beat herself up for the tiny flaws.

To her surprise, Miss Annette didn't beat her up, either.

"You'll find your stride again," her teacher said. It was probably the nicest Miss Annette had ever been to her. And then she added, "Just find it *quickly*."

Mikayla went through her audition routine for Drexton under her coach's scrutiny, Miss Annette punctuating the music with corrections like, "Leg up, elbow higher, posture, that's too rough, that's too soft. . . ."

And then, after she'd gone through the routine half a dozen times, she looked up, and Miss Annette wasn't there. Mikayla looked around, wondering for a second if she might have finally willed the coach away. And then she heard the woman's abrasive voice in the next room over.

Mikayla frowned, following it, and found Sara practicing a solo, Miss Annette scrutinizing her limbs and motions the way she'd done earlier with Mikayla.

Mikayla watched as Sara moved with elegance across the floor. She didn't make a single mistake. Sara had always been good, but recently, she'd gotten even *better*. But their next competition wasn't for weeks. Why did she have a new solo routine? What was it for? Sara finished at the same time as the music, coming to a stop in a graceful pose. In the mirror, Sara saw Mikayla watching, and smiled.

"How did it go?" asked Aria that night.

They were sitting on Mikayla's front stoop. Mikayla was icing her ankle while Aria cuddled Chow.

"Surprisingly okay. Miss Annette actually went easy on me."

"I didn't know Miss Annette *had* an easy setting."

"Me neither," said Mikayla, laughing. "So what did *you* do today?" she asked, feeling vaguely jealous of Aria's adventures, even before she heard about them.

Aria scratched Chow's head. "Just wandered, mostly. I love how big this city is. I love how, if you just start walking in any direction, you find something fascinating. Like this one place . . ."

Mikayla tried to listen, but her thoughts were already drifting back to Filigree. She couldn't stop thinking about Sara's routine, how *good* she'd been, and the smug way she'd looked at Mikayla.

Like she had a secret.

It wasn't until Friday that she found out what Sara's secret was.

After practice, Miss Annette dismissed the other dancers, but told Mikayla and Sara to stay behind.

"Girls," she said, clasping her hands. "My golden girls."

Mikayla frowned. That had always been Miss Annette's name for *her*.

"Tomorrow," she went on, "is an important day for both of you."

Mikayla felt herself freeze. *Both* of them?

"What do you mean?" asked Mikayla.

"Oh, you must have missed it while you were home sick," said Sara. "I got an invitation to audition at Drexton."

Mikayla's stomach turned. She looked to Miss Annette for an explanation. The invitations had all gone out weeks ago. Their teacher must have pulled strings to get Sara a last-minute chance.

"I couldn't exactly put all my eggs in one basket," explained Miss Annette, gesturing to Mikayla's ankle, "especially an injured one. My school has a reputation to maintain."

Mikayla swallowed hard. For the last *six years* a Filigree dancer had taken the coveted opening spot at Drexton, and Miss Annette obviously wasn't taking any chances. Which meant she no longer thought Mikayla was gold.

Sara's smile spread, and Mikayla felt tears burning her eyes. She didn't let them show, not even as she walked out of the studio, changed, and left with Sara.

"I guess we'll finally see what all those medals have bought you," said Sara when they were alone on the sidewalk. "Or if they were all a waste."

Mikayla fumed all the way to the subway.

She had always assumed *she* was Miss Annette's only candidate. It never occurred to her that Miss Annette would make sure Sara got an invitation.

Mikayla was the best dancer at Filigree. She'd sacrificed everything to *stay* the best.

But Sara had been working just as hard to close the gap. It wouldn't take much for them to switch places, for Mikayla to be the one walking away with silver. But for the Drexton audition, there was no silver, no second best. It was all or nothing.

She *couldn't* lose, not now.

She had to be best.

She had to be gold.

chapter 18

ARIA

Aria found Mikayla in her basement that night, soaked in sweat and grimacing every time she spun on her bad ankle.

"She's been down there all evening," Mikayla's mom had said as she opened the front door for Aria. "She won't come up. I know she's nervous about tomorrow, but still. You'd think it was a matter of life and death."

"I think to Mikayla it sometimes feels that way."

Now, Aria stood at the bottom of the stairs and watched Mikayla finish her routine.

Aria felt like the last week had never happened. The girl Mikayla had been, the one she was becoming again — fun-loving, whimsical — was gone, all Aria's progress washed away. What had happened?

The song ended, and Mikayla stood for a moment, breathless, before walking over to the music player and starting the song over. She took a pose and was about to go again when she saw Aria. She straightened, and the music played without her.

"Hey," said Aria.

"Hey," said Mikayla, clearly distracted.

"Why don't you take a break?" said Aria.

"I can't," said Mikayla.

"It's a nice night," pressed Aria, "and I bet you'll feel better if we —"

"I said I *can't*," protested Mikayla, her face hardening. "I need to practice. It's still not —"

"Perfect?" said Aria with a sad smile. "I thought we talked about that word."

"Not now, Aria," said Mikayla darkly.

Aria braved a step forward into the room. "Why are you so upset?"

When Mikayla didn't answer, Aria crossed the small room and put her hands on Mikayla's shoulders. "Look at me," she said, even though she wished she could say, "Look at you." She wished there was some kind of magic to show a person multiple versions of themselves, so Mikayla could see what all this pressure was doing to erase the beautiful, happy girl she'd become. "This is why you didn't want to go back, remember?"

But Mikayla shrugged her off. "I'm just nervous," she said.

"Well, all you can do is your best."

"But what if it's not good enough?" asked Mikayla, her voice on the edge of tears.

Aria held out her hands. "Then it wasn't meant to be."

Mikayla rubbed at her face, clearly frustrated. "Sara's auditioning."

Aria didn't understand. "So?"

"So she's *good*, Aria. She's amazing. And she hasn't spent the last week injured! She could take the spot at Drexton instead."

Aria sighed. "Maybe she *should*."

Mikayla gasped and put a hand to her cheek, as though Aria had hit her. "How can you *say* that?"

"I just mean" — Aria took a deep breath — "maybe it would be *better*. You don't *want* this, Mikayla. Not really." Once she started, she couldn't seem to stop. "I know you want to make your parents proud, but you don't want to go to Drexton, and you're going to be miserable if you get in, and you might be disappointed if you don't, but maybe then you'll accept that this isn't healthy, and finally give yourself a break. Not from dance, necessarily, but from *this*. The pressure and the feeling like nothing is good enough. Like *you're* not good enough. So, yeah," she said, looking Mikayla in the eye. "You're the best dancer I've ever seen, and there's no question you deserve to get into Drexton. But I think you deserve to be happy, too. So for that reason, I hope Sara gets the spot."

Mikayla stared at Aria long and hard. And then her face changed, morphed from sadness and frustration to *anger*. Her blue smoke was so thick it looked like it could choke someone.

"Get out," she snapped.

"Mikayla," started Aria, but the other girl threw up her hand and pointed at the door.

"You obviously don't get it. You're not helping anything, not helping *me*, so just *go away*."

Aria recoiled. She could *feel* Mikayla's order, the same way a person might feel a bucket of cold water. It was tangible, real, and Aria felt her shadow shift beneath her feet.

She retreated through the door and up the stairs, and the last thing she saw was Mikayla turning away before Aria's shadow came to life and swallowed her whole.

$\cdot \quad \cdot \quad \cdot$

Aria didn't know that someone could banish a guardian angel.

It wasn't the only time she'd been told to go away, but the first time it happened, with Gabby, she thought she'd disappeared out of sheer embarrassment. Now, as she sat on a bench in a subway station, she wondered if human girls had some magic of their own.

When the train came, Aria got on. She didn't know where she was going. She just wanted to be going somewhere. She'd spent quite a lot of time on the trains the last few nights, and something about the motion helped her think. Aria leaned her head back against the seat.

She wished there was something she could do to keep Mikayla from going to the audition, but she couldn't think of anything, besides pushing the girl down some stairs, and that didn't seem very angelic.

The problem, Aria was beginning to realize, was that even though Mikayla's accident had given her something that she needed — a break, a chance to step back — it had only been because of an *accident*. And if Aria had learned anything from helping Gabby and Caroline, and from *trying* to help Mikayla, it was that people had to *choose* change. Aria couldn't choose for them. When it came to whether or not to stop dancing, Mikayla needed to make the decision for herself.

Aria felt a pang in her chest. She'd felt it before, the sinking weight that came when someone she was trying to help was about to do something wrong, and she had to let them do it.

Because sometimes people had to make the wrong decision first, so they could make the right one later.

That was life, thought Aria. Choice after choice after choice, some of them wrong, and some of them right, and all of them important.

Aria told herself it would all work out. But the truth was, she didn't know what would happen. Didn't know how she could help change Mikayla's path.

And then she looked up and noticed another girl on the train. She looked to be a couple years older than Aria, maybe about fourteen or fifteen. She was pretty, with curly brown hair and a band of freckles across her nose.

The girl had big headphones on, music whispering out into the subway car. But that wasn't what caught Aria's attention.

No, it was the girl's charm bracelet, a red one, laced with a handful of tiny gold feathers.

Aria straightened in her seat when she saw it.

Because the girl wasn't just a girl.

She was an *angel*.

Aria thought of the teenage boy back in Gabby's hospital, the one with the green bracelet and the black feathers. She wondered how many kinds of angel there were. As many as there were colors in a box of crayons? Or more?

Aria wondered if this teenage angel was riding the subway just to think, like Aria, or if she was on her way to help someone.

And then, as the train slowed, the girl looked up, straight at Aria, and she winked.

Which wouldn't be that strange, except that Aria was invisible.

Aria sat there, stunned, as the girl stepped off the train. Then she found herself scrambling to her feet and following the girl out, ducking through the doors just before they slid shut. She trailed the girl through the subway station, up to the street and down the block, drawn along by some invisible rope, the same way she was pulled toward those she was supposed to help.

"Hey, wait!" Aria called, running to catch up.

But the girl rounded a corner, and by the time Aria rounded it, too, the other angel was gone, and she was alone on the street. Aria turned in a circle, looking for her, but the angel had simply vanished.

Aria stood there on the sidewalk, trying to get her

bearings. Where was she? What was she doing here? And then she heard the music overhead.

She looked up to see light two stories up, a row of floor-to-ceiling windows revealing an adult dance class.

Great, thought Aria. Just what she and Mikayla needed. More dance.

But something about this place was different. It wasn't like Filigree. The adults were dancing in pairs, spinning across the floor with their hands on waists and shoulders, smiling and laughing. Having fun.

The sign in front said PARK SLOPE COMMUNITY DANCE CENTER.

Aria climbed a short set of steps to the front door, where a poster announced:

ALL AGES WELCOME.

ALL LEVELS WELCOME.

UNDER 13 DANCE FREE UP TO 4X/WEEK.

A folder taped to the wall by the door held pamphlets, and Aria took one, opening it to find a calendar listing different classes on different days. Everything from jazz to modern to hip-hop and freestyle. On the back of the brochure was a quote from the owner, a woman named Philippa Rask.

Dance is expression, it read. *Dance is motion and emotion. There are no mistakes, so long as you dance what you feel.*

Aria smiled.

Maybe she'd been wrong. Maybe this was *exactly* what Mikayla needed.

Aria pocketed a brochure. Then she looked over her shoulder, half expecting the girl with the freckles and the red bracelet to be standing there.

Aria didn't know if guardian angels had guardian angels of their own. But if they did, she had a feeling she'd met hers tonight.

chapter 19

MIKAYLA

The day of the Drexton audition, Mikayla woke up feeling horrible. Her body ached from practicing too long — her shoulders were stiff, her legs sore, her ankle tender. But she felt even worse about yelling at Aria. Mikayla was still annoyed at her friend for not understanding, but her head was also full of thoughts and questions and fears.

She couldn't afford to think about failing, or her dad's unemployment, or the boxes, which just kept multiplying. Nor could she think about the fact that maybe she was mad at Aria because Aria was *right*.

She couldn't afford to think about anything but Drexton.

Her mom tried to get her to eat breakfast, but she wasn't hungry. She took a few bites of French toast and fed the rest to Chow, who seemed perfectly happy to take it off her hands. Her dad, normally hunched over his laptop, was dressed and ready to go. He and her mom would be accompanying Mikayla to the audition.

They took the subway into Manhattan, Mikayla's stomach in a knot the whole time. Before she knew it, they were walking down Broadway toward Drexton Academy.

"You're quiet, hon," said her mom, rubbing her shoulder.

Mikayla managed a smile. "Just nervous."

"You've got this," said her mom.

"You're going to do great," said her dad.

Finally Mikayla said, "It's not the end of the world, if I don't get in." Her voice was quiet and shaky.

"You will," said her dad.

"But if I don't —"

"It's okay to be nervous," said her mom. "But think positive."

Mikayla opened and closed her mouth to say something, but it was clear they wouldn't hear her.

"Just stay focused."

"Listen to the music."

"Make us proud."

"We're already proud."

"We're *always* proud."

Mikayla swallowed as they reached the steps of Drexton.

It loomed overhead, a large white stone building with its emblem — a cursive *D* and *A* intertwined to look like dancers locked in an embrace — on a marble pillar out front.

Beneath the dancing letters ran the Drexton Academy motto:

EAT SLEEP BREATHE DANCE.

The first three words were set in smaller type above the fourth, to emphasize the last word's importance.

And leaning up against that pillar, beneath the motto, was a girl whose hair shone copper in the sunlight. Aria! She was dressed in her usual colorful style — green pants and a purple-and-blue striped shirt.

Mikayla expected to feel anger rising up in her chest, but she was surprised to feel a sudden wave of relief instead.

"What are you doing here?" she cried.

Aria smiled. "I wanted to come and wish you good luck."

Mikayla crossed her arms. "Do you still want Sara to win?"

Aria's smile softened, but didn't disappear. "I want *you* to be happy," she said. "So if this is what you want, if winning the spot here will make that happen, then I hope you get it." She sounded like she really meant it. "I believe in you."

Mikayla looked down at their feet. The laces on her sneakers were white. Aria's were purple. "I'm sorry I got so mad at you," Mikayla whispered.

"It's all right," said Aria, and something about those three simple words helped Mikayla breathe again. Then Aria surprised her by throwing her arms around Mikayla's shoulders. Mikayla felt something well up in her, her fear and her doubts and everything she couldn't afford to face. She swallowed hard.

"Mikayla," said her mom. "We better get inside."

Mikayla pulled away. "I have to go."

"Can I come over after?" asked Aria.

"Yeah," said Mikayla.

Aria smiled. "Good luck," she said, stepping out of the way. "I'll see you on the other side."

The holding room was *packed*.

Mikayla hadn't expected there to be *so many* other kids, girls and boys, all warming up, all waiting, and wanting. Their nervous energy and their stretching made a kind of rhythm in the room. *Tap tap woosh.* They were all contemporary dancers, like Mikayla, and they were all *good*.

How many spots had Drexton opened up? One? Two? Three?

Suddenly Mikayla realized that Sara wasn't the only one she had to beat.

As if on cue, she spotted the other Filigree girl across the room, her blond hair pinned back, wearing her signature green leotard. She watched as Sara did a quadruple pirouette, nailing the turn Mikayla had struggled over. Their eyes met, and Sara smiled tightly.

Mikayla's stomach jumped just as a man in a suit and a thin woman with a bun appeared before a set of wooden doors.

The man had a walking stick and he rapped it against the marble floor, the sharp sound echoing even in the crowded space.

"Parents, friends, and anyone who's not auditioning today, please wait in the foyer. Dancers, stay here."

Mikayla's parents gave her a last hug and a kiss and retreated into the outer room. Mikayla was secretly glad when they were gone. Her face was starting to hurt from holding up the smile, and the moment they were out the door she let it fall away,

"Gather round," said the twiglike woman. "You've all been invited to audition today for a spot here at Drexton. When your name is called, you will come through this door behind us, introduce yourself, turn on your music, and perform your piece."

"But before we begin calling names," said the man, "we want all of you to understand what it means to be a Drexton dancer. As our motto suggests, we expect our performers to *eat*, *sleep*, and *breathe* dance. Every moment of the day. Every day of the week. That is the kind of dedication it takes to make it in this industry. And there's always someone ready to take your place."

Mikayla's chest tightened. Aria's voice echoed in her head. *What happens once you get in?*

"If you do not have what it takes," cut in the woman, "leave." No one moved. The man and woman smiled, even though they didn't seem happy. "Very well, let's begin."

Mikayla stood against the far wall, watching as dancer after dancer vanished into the audition room, the crowd thinning. When Sara was called, Mikayla forced herself to go over and wish her good luck. She'd expected a snarky reply, but Sara must have been just as scared as Mikayla was, because she only said, "You too."

Then it happened. "Mikayla Stevens!" the woman with the clipboard shouted. Her name had been called.

This was it.

Mikayla was terrified, and she realized in that moment, just before she pushed open the doors, that she didn't know what she was more afraid of: messing up or getting in.

Gold, she told herself, glancing down at her shimmery leotard. This was everything she'd worked for. Everything that mattered.

As Mikayla pushed the doors open, she noticed the Drexton Academy motto carved into the wood.

EAT SLEEP BREATHE DANCE.

In her head she heard, *Every moment of the day. Every day of the week.*

Only gold girls go to Drexton.

Make us proud.

You don't want this.

I don't have a choice.

You always have a choice.

She carried the voices — Drexton's and Miss Annette's and her parents' and Aria's and her own — with her, all their hope and expectation. Mikayla felt it all wrap around her, weigh her down.

Beyond the doors was a dance studio, wood-paneled floors and a mirrored wall. The admissions committee — the thin woman and the man with the cane, as well as a young man with a mustache and an older woman — sat behind a large table, waiting.

Mikayla padded into the center of the room and introduced herself, and the committee stared at her over their papers.

She could hear her pulse pounding in her ears as she went to the speakers, plugged in her iPod, and hit PLAY, then retreated back to her place and took her pose.

After a few seconds that felt like *forever*, the music finally started.

But Mikayla didn't.

In that moment, her whole mind went blank. Her body froze.

She knew the routine backward and forward and upside down, but standing there, in front of the admissions committee, her limbs went numb. The hesitation only lasted a moment, but it was a moment too long.

By the time Mikayla started dancing, she was off-tempo, a step behind the music.

She couldn't catch up.

She faltered on a kick.

She fell out of a turn.

She felt every inch of her body, and knew it wasn't working.

When the song finally ended and Mikayla toddled to a stop, she felt sick.

She had performed hundreds of times — *hundreds* — in front of thousands of people, and she'd never, ever choked. Why did she have to choke *today*?

She'd messed up, beyond repair. She could see it in the admissions committee's crossed arms. Their tight mouths. Their hovering pens.

Mikayla stood before them breathless, hopeless, heartbroken.

"You can go now," said the woman with the bun.

"Have a nice day," said the man with the mustache.

"We'll be in touch," added the man with the cane.

"Next!" called the older woman.

Mikayla gave a single, tight bow, and backed out of the room.

It was over.

She'd failed.

"Well?" asked her mom excitedly when she came outside.

"How'd it go?" asked her dad, opening his arms for a hug.

But Mikayla said nothing, only shrugged.

"Mikayla?" pressed her mom, looking worried. "What happened?"

"I don't know," she whispered.

"I'm sure you were fine," said her dad.

Mikayla shook her head. She felt her eyes burning.

"It's okay, honey," said her mom.

"It's okay," echoed her dad.

But it wasn't okay. How could they think it was okay?

She'd failed. Failed them, failed Miss Annette, failed herself.

On the subway ride home, she kept her lips pressed together. She could hear her parents whispering, but she pretended not to hear.

"I just need some time alone," she said as soon as they got home, and they let her go.

She went straight to the basement studio and shut the door.

It was over.

It was all over.

She'd had her chance, and she'd ruined it.

She looked at herself in the mirrored surface, eyes puffy from held-back tears, a wall of gold at her back.

And then she turned, picked up one of those trophies,

and threw it against the ground as hard as she could. It broke into several pieces, skidding across the floor. She took up a medal and chucked it at the mirror, splintering the glass. And then she picked up and threw down another trophy, and another, and another, until everything else was ruined, too.

chapter 20

ARIA

Aria found Mikayla sitting on the floor, surrounded by her broken trophies.

She'd cleared the shelves in the room of every single prize.

Aria had seen everything, of course (being invisible had its perks). She'd watched the audition, which was pretty disastrous, and Mikayla's sullen reaction to her parents. She could feel the breakdown coming like a wave, and she'd let it break.

Now she stood in the studio, visible again, while Mikayla sat on the floor, staring at her splintered reflection in the broken mirror. Her smoke swirled heavy and blue around her shoulders.

"What do you want, Aria?"

"To help," she replied, stepping carefully around the mess of broken trophies and cast-away medals.

Mikayla looked up, her eyes red. "I choked," she said. "After everything, all that work, all that worrying . . . it was all for nothing."

"I doubt that," said Aria, sitting down beside Mikayla with her back against the wall, so their shoulders and knees bumped together. "Nothing is for nothing."

Mikayla shook her head and looked down at the years of trophies littering the floor. "I just thought . . . if I could get through the audition . . . but I saw the motto and I panicked."

"Eat, Sleep, Breathe Dance," recited Aria.

Mikayla tipped her head back and wiped her nose on her sleeve. "You were right. Going to Drexton was a bad idea. But I couldn't not go, either. There was no way to win."

Aria leaned her shoulder against Mikayla's. "Not everything in life can be divided into win and lose. Which is probably a good thing. But it means having to make choices. Some of them hard."

Mikayla looked around. "When did everything get so messy?" she asked, and Aria knew she wasn't talking about the trashed studio.

"It's going to be okay," said Aria. "We can fix this."

"How?" whispered Mikayla, and Aria knew she was finally ready to listen.

Aria got up and picked up two pieces of a broken trophy. Then she knelt in front of Mikayla. "Anything can be fixed," she said. "If you know how to put it back together."

As she said it, she fitted the halves of the trophy together, one into the other. There was a small flash of light, and an instant later, the trophy was whole again. She held it up for Mikayla to see.

Mikayla's eyes grew wide with disbelief.

"How — how — did you . . ." she stammered.

"I told you," said Aria with a bright smile. "I'm here to help. But I guess I should explain. . . ."

Mikayla's face was frozen in shock. "A guardian angel . . ."

Aria nodded. "*Your* guardian angel, specifically."

Mikayla shook her head so hard her bun loosened. "Come on. You actually expect me to believe that?"

"You told me that you used to believe in lots of things," Aria pointed out.

"When I was a *kid*. And then I grew up and realized they weren't real."

Aria gestured to the repaired trophy. "I'm real."

"But that doesn't mean you're an angel." Mikayla blinked, and hugged herself. "Maybe I'm going crazy."

"You're not," Aria assured. She was making her way around the studio. She held up another broken statue, and fixed it with another flash of light. "You saw me do that, right?"

"I guess. I have no idea. How did you do it?"

"Magic."

"Magic doesn't exist," said Mikayla flatly.

"Of course it does," said Aria, setting the mended trophy on the shelf. "I told you, the world is big and strange and full of wonder. Is it really so hard to believe in me?"

"Actually, yeah, it kind of is."

Aria brought her hand to the broken mirror, and the cracks across the front traced backward. It was pretty cool — Aria hadn't been totally sure she *could* mend things until she'd magicked the trophy back into one piece (it would have been awkward if that hadn't worked).

Mikayla watched silently, her head tipped to the side. "How am I *supposed* to believe you're my guardian angel?" she challenged.

Aria wasn't surprised that Mikayla was resisting her. She thought of the best way to explain.

"Think about it, Mikayla. I just . . ." She made a *poof* motion with her hands. ". . . appeared in your life, right when you needed me. At the competition, at the school, at Filigree. I wasn't here, and then I was. Do you honestly think it's a coincidence?"

Mikayla made a noncommittal *hmm* sound. And then she squinted at her.

"I guess it kind of makes sense," she said at last.

"Really?" said Aria, brightening.

Mikayla gave a wan smile. "No, I mean, it's still totally crazy, but I guess it makes sense in a crazy kind of way. It makes *you* make sense. The way you just showed up in my life. The way you always know what to say. And the way you dance. I guess we really were supposed to cross paths."

Aria nodded. "I thought you'd be excited," she said. "I mean, I'm basically proof that magic is real! Score one for Young Mikayla."

"Does that mean monsters are real, too?" Aria could see the flicker of light in Mikayla's eyes, some old part of her shining through the skepticism. "Dragons and fairies and stuff like that?"

Aria chewed her lip. "I have no idea. I've never met one. But who knows? Maybe one day I will. Or you will."

Mikayla frowned. "Why didn't you just tell me what you were?"

Aria set another trophy back on the shelf. "Would that have made you listen?" Mikayla bit her lip. Aria smiled. "You couldn't see past Drexton until you *got past Drexton*."

At the mention of the academy, Mikayla groaned. "Ugh, I can't believe I bombed the audition." She looked up sharply. "Wait, if you're really my guardian angel . . ."

"I am," said Aria, suddenly nervous. She'd seen that kind of excitement before, and it was usually followed by a bad idea.

"Then can't you use magic to go back and change it? Make it so I didn't mess up?"

There it was. Aria laughed. "I'm an angel, not a time-traveler," she said. "And even if I could change the past," she went on, "I wouldn't."

"What about my dad?" asked Mikayla, urgently.

"What about him?"

"Can you help him? Can you use your magic to get him his job back?"

Aria's heart sank. "I'm sorry, but I can't."

"Why not?"

"He's not the one who needs my help," she said. "You are. And I can't fix people's problems." Mikayla looked devastated.

"Not even for you. Only *you* can fix your problems. But I can help you."

Mikayla drew her knees up to her chest and wrapped her arms around them, but she nodded. "Okay."

"Okay." Aria was quiet, watching Mikayla. She could see that some part of the other girl was starting to believe in her. "So, the question," said Aria, "the smallest, biggest, simplest, hardest question is this: What are we going to do about dance?"

Mikayla put her head on her knees. "I honestly don't know."

Aria put her hand on the girl's shoulder. "I think you do."

Mikayla sighed and wiped her eyes. "I guess I'll have to quit. I don't *want* to," she said. "But without the Drexton scholarship, my parents can't afford to keep paying for my classes. So it doesn't make sense."

"What if money weren't a factor?"

"Money is always a factor."

"But what if it weren't? What if dance were free, and it was just about whether or not you *wanted* to do it? Then what would you do?"

Mikayla's eyes went to a set of photos on the wall by the door. In among the more recent pictures were a few older ones from the album she'd found, in which a young Mikayla posed with a group of girls, all in matching blue outfits. The young Mikayla beamed, not a fake smile, but a real, delighted one.

"I meant it when I said that I missed dancing," she said, "the way it used to be. Back when it wasn't about hitting every mark, or being the best, or winning gold. It was just . . . fun. Freeing."

"Okay," said Aria, standing up. "So we need to make it about the dance again."

"You make it sound so easy."

"Maybe it is," said Aria. "Maybe it *can* be. If you're willing to give it a try."

Mikayla's smoke tangled around her, but Aria could see, woven through it, a tired but persistent hope. Her eyes had lit up when she'd talked about dance the way it used to be.

For once, Aria had to help someone back instead of forward.

"I have an idea," Aria said. "You only have to do one thing."

"What's that?" asked Mikayla.

"Will you trust me?" Aria asked.

Mikayla hesitated, gazing around the studio, now put back together as if nothing had happened. And then she nodded. "I trust you."

"Okay," Aria said. "I'll come back here tomorrow to pick you up. And you'll see."

chapter 21

MIKAYLA

"I don't know about this, Aria."

"Come on, Mikayla. You said you'd trust me."

They were standing on a sidewalk in front of a building marked PARK SLOPE COMMUNITY DANCE CENTER.

"I did say that," said Mikayla. "But I didn't say I'd join another dance academy."

"This isn't a dance academy," Aria said. "It's a *community dance center*." She accentuated every word. "And my advice is to try it. One class. If you don't like it, you don't have to go back."

It wasn't just the thought of dancing in the wake of yesterday's failure that made Mikayla's stomach twist. It was Filigree. If Miss Annette found out that she was taking lessons somewhere else —

As if she could read her mind — was that a thing guardian angels could do? — Aria said, "It's Sunday. You wouldn't be at Filigree anyway, so it's not like you're cheating."

Aria started up the steps, but Mikayla still hesitated. Aria looked back.

"You told me you miss the way dance used to be. No pressure. No expectation. That's what this is. So give it a shot. You might enjoy it. Besides, it's free!"

Mikayla took a deep breath. She did want to get back to that kind of dancing that made the world fall away. She wasn't sure if she *could* find her way back, but she knew she could try. She owed Aria that much.

"Trust me," said Aria with a mischievous grin. "I'm your guardian angel, after all."

Mikayla laughed — she'd been up most of the night, seesawing between belief and disbelief about Aria — but she climbed the steps. Aria held the door open for her, and the two went in.

Inside, the dance center was alive with noise and motion.

A man at the front desk smiled warmly. "Morning, girls. Here for the one o'clock class?"

Aria nodded. "We're new here. I'm afraid we don't know where to start."

The man produced two small slips of paper. "Start with these. Your passes," he said. "You're both under thirteen, right? So you get four free classes a week." He punched a hole out of each card. "Just keep these with you. The studio is through these doors."

"Anything else we should know?" asked Aria.

The man smiled. "Just have fun."

Mikayla quickly discovered that the Community Dance Center was *very* different from Filigree. Different from any dance class she'd ever taken. First of all, the dancers ranged in age from nine and ten to late teens, and in experience from beginners to, well, Mikayla. She didn't recognize any of the dancers from competitions, but she supposed that made sense. A handful of adults lounged in a low set of wooden bleachers at the side of the studio, but everyone else was on the floor, casually warming up.

The instructor, Miss Rask ("Just call me Phillipa," she said), was middle-aged, with long hair coiled in a loose braid around her head. She was tall and lithe, built like a prima ballerina, but there was a relaxation to the way she held herself.

"Hello, everyone," she said when it was time to start. Mikayla's heart fluttered nervously. "I see we've got a couple new faces." She nodded at Aria and Mikayla. "Welcome." She held a remote in one hand, and when she pressed a button, the room filled with soft music. "Let's get started. . . ."

The warm-ups were easy: basic stretches, calisthenics. Mikayla did each movement quickly, almost automatically. She noticed Aria stretching and looking content. *My guardian angel*, Mikayla thought, observing her. No wonder Aria seemed to give off light wherever she went. It all added up now.

Next, Phillipa began teaching everyone a routine. She demonstrated a handful of steps, linking one into the next, and then everyone would repeat them back a few times until they got the hang of them. Meanwhile, Phillipa would walk around and help.

Mikayla picked the steps up within her first two tries, so she was surprised when Phillipa stopped beside her.

"Did I do it wrong?" asked Mikayla, nervously.

Phillipa smiled. "No," she said. "But you dance like you're afraid of messing up." She took her by one arm, and shook the limb slightly. "Relax," she said kindly. "Don't worry about it. Just let go."

Phillipa held on to Mikayla until she physically felt her shoulders loosening, her breath moving more smoothly. When the instructor let go, and Mikayla did the move again, it came easily. It wasn't perfect, but it felt right. Good.

Mikayla's heart raced, but this time with excitement. How long had it been since dancing *felt good*?

Phillipa had everyone dance the segment, then moved on to a second, and a third, stringing them together each time, slowly building something bigger.

More than anything, stressed Phillipa in between segments, you had to listen to the music. "Every single time you dance, it's going to be different, but as long as you move with the music, instead of against it, you'll be fine."

Mikayla had never thought of it that way, but it made sense. How long had she been moving against the music? Fighting it, and her body, like they were a current?

As the class neared its end — how had the two hours gone so quickly? — Phillipa had them string all the segments of dance together and run the entire routine from start to finish. And to Mikayla's surprise — and delight — something clicked. The music filled her head and the room fell away.

She felt the way she had back when she first started dancing. Happy. Free.

When the music stopped, Mikayla realized she was smiling. A real, genuine smile. She stole a look at Aria, who was beaming triumphantly, as if she could see the change in her.

The class did the whole routine three more times, more and more students finding their stride, and by the end of the third, Mikayla was breathless, but giddy. How could Filigree and this feel so different? How could they both be called *dance*?

"Good job, everyone!" called Phillipa. To Mikayla's surprise, the instructor applauded, and the other students applauded back, the room momentarily swallowed by the sound.

The class broke apart, and Mikayla followed Aria outside.

"Well?" said Aria. "That wasn't so bad, was it? I thought —"

Mikayla surprised both of them by throwing her arms around her guardian angel.

"Thank you," she said into the angel's shoulder.

"You're welcome," said Aria. "Just doing my job."

Mikayla's excitement about the new dance class followed her home, but it died the moment she and Aria stepped inside.

Her father was hunched at the kitchen table, her mother whispering to him, and Mikayla could tell that yet another job had fallen through.

Doubled over like that, he looked broken, and Aria tugged her away by the arm, the two retreating to Mikayla's room.

"I wish there was something I could do for my dad," Mikayla said, shutting the door.

"There is," said Aria, and Mikayla brightened before the angel added, "Be there for him."

"That's not what I meant."

"But it is what you can do," said Aria.

"But maybe if I had gotten into Drexton . . ." said Mikayla, but she trailed off, knowing that it wouldn't have fixed everything. As much as she wanted there to be a simple solution, there wasn't one. "He just used to be such a happy person," said Mikayla. "Now he's always on edge."

"That sounds familiar," said Aria with a smile.

"What do you mean?"

"Well, *you* used to be happy, too. Until you became so afraid of letting everyone down. That's probably how he feels. The same way you're scared of disappointing your parents, he's probably scared of disappointing you."

Mikayla had never thought of it like that.

She slumped back against the bed, but Aria got up to go.

"Hey. Where do you go at night?" Mikayla asked. "Do you just disappear until I need you again?"

Aria shook her head. "Sometimes I'm *invisible*, but I'm still real. Mostly I explore the city. I want to see everything."

"People live here for years and still don't see it all," said Mikayla.

"That's okay," said Aria. "I want to see as much as I can before . . ." she trailed off, frowned, and picked back up. "Before I'm done."

"How will you know when you're done?" asked Mikayla when Aria was at the door. Mikayla felt a stab of worry. She didn't want Aria to not be a part of her life anymore.

Aria looked down at her bracelet. "I'll know," she said. "But we're not done yet."

Mikayla watched the door close behind the girl, and swore she saw Aria *disappear* as she stepped through. She sat there a moment, staring at the poster on the back of the door.

WINNERS NEVER QUIT. QUITTERS NEVER WIN.

Mikayla got up and took the poster down. She rolled it up and tucked it in one of the moving boxes. It was a small step in the right direction.

Then she went to find her father.

He was still sitting at the kitchen table, typing away, and Mikayla wrapped her arms lightly around his shoulders.

"Hey, honey," he said, distracted.

At first Mikayla didn't know what to say. But if Aria was right, her dad really felt the same way she did, so she told him what she'd want to hear.

"I'm proud of you," she said. "No matter what happens."

At that, he stopped typing and looked up, his eyes shining with tears. "Even if we have to move?"

Mikayla could almost feel Aria there with her, a touch on her arm, as she said, "A house is just a house. Home is the people in it."

Mikayla went back to her room feeling lighter than she had in ages. For the first time, the boxes didn't scare her.

chapter 22

ARIA

Aria had made quite a dent in her to-do list, and yet it wasn't getting any shorter.

Every time she crossed an item off, two more seemed to pop up. Mikayla was right, there was just too much to see, even if someone had a whole life in which to see it.

But Aria didn't. Mikayla's smoke was thinning, which meant Aria was running out of time.

"Where did you come from?" Mikayla asked Aria as they rode the subway to school that Monday.

"I told you, California," said Aria.

"Why California?"

"I was helping a girl named Caroline."

Mikayla swung her legs back and forth on the subway seat. "What was her problem?"

"Bullies."

"And who did you help before that?"

"Gabby. Her brother was sick."

"And before that?"

Aria shrugged. "Gabby was the first girl I helped." She held out her bracelet for Mikayla to see. "See these rings?" she said. "I get a feather for each girl I help." She touched the silver feather that belonged to Gabby, then the linked silver feathers from Caroline and Lily. And then the empty ring. "This one is you."

Mikayla frowned. "What happens after me? Where will you go when you're done?"

It was a question that Gabby had asked, as well as Caroline. But with those girls, Aria had known what to say — *to the next girl who needs my help* — and now she didn't.

"I don't know," she admitted. "Wherever I'm supposed to be."

Mikayla nodded thoughtfully, and Aria was grateful when she changed the subject. "So," Mikayla said cheerfully, "were you able to get through any of your math problems?"

Aria was pleased that Mikayla seemed to be in bright spirits all day. Up until lunch, that is, when they took their seats

and Beth said, "OMG, I texted you but didn't hear back —
how was the Drexton audition?"

The natural smile slid from Mikayla's mouth, her smoke
twitching and twisting. "I don't know," she said. "I don't
think it went well."

"No way. I'm sure you did great," said Katie.

"You're just being hard on yourself," Beth chimed in.

Mikayla looked down at her food and managed a nod.
Then she felt Aria squeeze her arm. "To be honest," she said,
"I'm kind of relieved. I'm not sure it's what I wanted. Anyway,
it's not the end of the world. One way or another."

Beth gaped at Aria. "What have you done with Mikayla
Stevens?" she teased. Aria smiled, picking up an apple from
her lunch tray.

"Speaking of body snatchers," said Katie. "There's a
Broadway show opening on Friday, all about aliens. We
should get tickets."

Mikayla went quiet. "I can't," she said at last.

"Filigree?" asked Katie, in a voice that made it clear they
were used to this excuse.

"No," said Mikayla. And then, after another deep breath,
she said, "Money's really tight right now. I can't afford it."

Aria held her hand under the table, knowing how hard it
was for Mikayla to finally be honest about her circumstances.

She was tense, obviously worried about how the girls would react.

But Kate simply said, "Okay, no worries." And Beth added, "Let's do something free, then. There's a concert in Central Park. . . ."

And just like that, the conversation — and the world — went on.

Mikayla squeezed Aria's hand back, and let go. "Sounds great," she said.

The last bell rang, and Mikayla and Aria grabbed their things and made their way outside.

Sara was a few strides ahead, already heading for Filigree. But she looked back, saw Mikayla, and stopped, obviously waiting. Aria skipped down the stairs and took a few steps in the other direction. Toward the subway that would take them to the Community Dance Center.

This was the moment of truth.

Mikayla stood there between them, at the literal intersection of two paths.

Aria hadn't said anything, hadn't tried to tell her what she thought was right. It had to be *her* choice. Go back to Filigree, and everything that came with it — the hours of training, the harsh criticism, the kind of dance that won medals and left her feeling hollowed out. Or go to the Community Dance Center and . . . dance. No gold trophies, no prestige, but no pressure, either.

Mikayla didn't have to decide for forever, but for now.

"Aren't you coming?" asked Sara, impatiently.

Mikayla hesitated, and looked from one girl to the other. Then she shook her head.

"Not today," she told Sara. "You go on ahead."

And then she took another step in the right direction.

chapter 23

MIKAYLA

"Welcome back," said Phillipa, holding the door open.

Mikayla and Aria stood there, breathless from running, ready to dance.

And for two hours, everything was perfect. Not perfect in the technical, no-points-lost kind of way, but perfect in the simple, wonderful way that comes with doing something that you love. And Mikayla did love it. She was remembering *how* to love it.

There was one thing, though, that caught Mikayla by surprise. She'd gotten there, ready to revisit the dance from the day before, but Phillipa never brought it back. Instead she taught the class something new. And it was great, half-full of moves Mikayla had never tried before, but it left her with a question.

When the class broke apart, she approached Phillipa at the front of the room, Aria trailing behind.

"Ah," said the woman, "my little Filigree."

Mikayla was startled. "How did you know?"

Phillipa smiled. "The way you danced yesterday," she said. "And the fact it's on your jacket."

Mikayla realized she was wearing her competition jacket, and felt silly.

"What's your name?" asked Phillipa.

"Mikayla," she said. "And this is Aria. And I was just wondering, when do we perform?"

Phillipa gave her a quizzical smile. "We don't, dear."

Mikayla's brow crinkled. "Then what's the point of learning a routine?"

"The point?" Phillipa tapped a finger on her chin. "Well, my dear, I imagine it's to grow, to stretch, and to have fun."

Mikayla saw Aria break into a smile that seemed to brighten all the lights overhead.

"Oh," said Mikayla.

"Each class, you learn a routine," explained Phillipa. "You spend the whole class with it. Embrace it. Enjoy it. And then you let it go."

"But . . . why?"

"We let it go because it served its purpose, Mikayla. This isn't a class for the audience. This is a class for the dancer. Does that make sense?"

Mikayla nodded. After years of competition, that idea would take time to sink in. But she was willing to try.

When Mikayla got home, her mom was making dinner.

"How was dance?" she asked, and Mikayla felt a pang of guilt as she said, "It was fine." She knew she'd have to tell her, but couldn't bring herself to do it. What if she got mad? What if she made Mikayla go back to Filigree?

"Sit down," said her mom, and for an instant, Mikayla thought she knew, that she could see it in her eyes. But when Mikayla slid into the nearest chair, her mom said, "Are you ready to talk about Drexton?"

Mikayla looked down. She hadn't been able to bring herself to say it, but now she took a breath and said, "I choked."

"Was it your ankle?" asked her mom. "If it was bothering you, maybe we could ask for a redo or —"

Mikayla shook her head. "It wasn't my ankle. I just panicked and I . . . I blew it. I'm sorry."

Her mom wrapped her arms around her. "Don't be. We all stumble. The important thing is getting back up. If you keep working hard, I bet Miss Annette can get you another chance and then —"

"Mom, I . . ." she cut in, and then trailed off. Silence hung in place of the truth. *There's something I need to tell you*, she wanted to say. *I don't want to compete anymore.* But all that came out was, "I'm tired. I better go finish my homework before dinner."

Then she escaped to her room.

"When are you going to tell them?" asked a voice as she shut the door. Mikayla jumped and saw Aria standing there. Being a guardian angel apparently came with the ability to sneak up on people.

"Soon," said Mikayla. Saying it out loud — *I'm quitting* — would make it so real, so final.

As if Aria could read her mind, she said, "Try not to think of it as quitting. It's just changing course."

Mikayla swallowed, and nodded. "I'll tell them tomorrow."

But Mikayla didn't tell them tomorrow. Or the next day.

Every day, after school, she and Aria hit the front steps of Coleridge, and Sara went toward Filigree and Mikayla didn't. Every day she and Aria went to the Community Dance Center and had a great time, so great that all the way home Mikayla would say that was it, she'd decided, and tonight she was going to tell her parents. And every night she'd get home and her dad would be worried or her mom would be tense and she'd chicken out. She was stuck in a cycle of doubt.

Then, on Thursday, everything changed.

She got home and found her father at the kitchen table, hugging her mother.

He was crying, and a horrible pit formed in Mikayla's stomach until she realized that he wasn't sad. He was *happy*.

"What's going on?" she asked, and he pulled her into the family hug.

"I got a job," he said, his voice shaky. "It won't pay nearly as well as the old job, but it's something."

Mikayla felt her whole chest lighten, even under his embrace, and as she pulled away, she thought, *This is it.* This was the right time to tell them, when they were relaxed and relieved.

As the celebration died down, she said, "Mom, Dad, there's something I need to tell you. . . ."

"What is it?" asked her mom.

Mikayla hesitated. "It's about dance. . . ." she started.

But she didn't get a chance to explain, because just then the phone rang.

It was Miss Annette.

And she was *furious*.

chapter 24

ARIA

In the end, it was Aria's fault.

By Thursday, the secret was still tangled in Mikayla's smoke, and Aria was starting to think she would never tell her parents.

She couldn't push Mikayla over the threshold, couldn't use plain words or magic to force her to change. But sometimes, Aria realized, when someone won't seek out change, you have to bring the change to them.

It had started with Sara after school.

Aria beat Mikayla to the front steps, where Sara was waiting, as she had been every day. "Is she coming?" asked Sara impatiently.

When Aria shook her head, Sara frowned. "Well, quitters never win."

"She's not a quitter," said Aria.

"Could have fooled me," snapped Sara.

"She hasn't stopped *dancing*," said Aria. "Just because she's taking a break from Filigree."

Sara's eyes narrowed, and she opened her mouth to say something, when Mikayla showed up, eyes bright with excitement, obviously eager to get going.

"Ready?" Mikayla asked.

"Ready," said Aria.

As they made their way to the Community Dance Center, Aria could feel Sara following, but she didn't look back.

Now she sat perched on the Stevenses' couch, invisible legs crossed, waiting for the call or the knock or whatever it would be.

She'd been shocked when Mikayla actually started to tell her parents herself. And then the phone had rung. Because of course Sara had told Miss Annette.

Mrs. Stevens answered the phone and Aria listened intently. "Why hello, Miss Annette. How can I . . ." she trailed off, then frowned. "No, I *didn't* know that Mikayla hadn't been at Filigree all week." She shot a look at Mikayla, who shrank away. "Well, I'm sure there's an explanation . . . Excuse me? No, I've no idea why she would go there . . . No one is going behind anyone's back . . . Well, obviously there's a reason . . . Yes, I'll be sure to find out."

And with that, Mrs. Stevens hung up the phone. Aria saw Mikayla watching her mother with trepidation.

"What was that about?" asked Mikayla's father.

"That," her mom said slowly, "was Miss Annette. Apparently Mikayla hasn't been to class all week." She turned to her daughter. "What's going on?"

Mikayla stood there, rocking back and forth on her heels.

"Mikayla," said her father sternly, and Aria got up, walked over, and put her invisible hand gently on the girl's shoulder, for strength.

At her touch, Mikayla exhaled and then said, "I've been going to classes somewhere else. A community dance center. It's open to everyone, and it's free."

"You're not quitting dance," her father said sternly. "I didn't raise a quitter."

Mikayla cringed at the word. "It's not quitting," she said. "It's just changing direction."

"But why?" asked her mom. "You've worked so hard —"

"Because . . . I stopped loving it."

"You're upset about Drexton," said her dad. "That's natural. But —"

"It's not just the audition," said Mikayla.

"Where is this coming from?" pressed her mom.

"Filigree is expensive," Mikayla said, "and I'm not having fun."

But her father only seemed to hear the first part. "We'll find the money. We'll make it work. Especially now —"

"But I don't want to make it work," Mikayla pressed on, sounding stronger than Aria had ever heard her. "I don't want to compete anymore. I don't want to focus on every flaw. I don't want to spend every minute of every day worried about being the best, stressed out by the idea of getting silver instead of gold." Her voice cracked, and tears slid down her face. "Winning isn't worth it if you're miserable. And I've been miserable for a long time. I'm sorry if I'm letting you down. I'm sorry if this makes me a failure."

As the words poured out into the air, so did the smoke, uncoiling from Mikayla's shoulders and dissolving into fog and air and nothing. Aria watched it happen.

Only the barest tendril remained as Mikayla stood facing her parents. Finally, they both folded her into a hug.

"You're our daughter," said her mom. "Of course we don't think that."

"Why didn't you say anything before?" asked her dad.

Mikayla wiped her eyes. "I'm sorry. I didn't want to disappoint you."

"We're only disappointed that you didn't tell us you were so miserable," her dad said softly.

"You've given up so much . . ." Mikayla started.

"We didn't give it up for you to be a star," said her dad. "We gave it up for you to be *happy*."

"So this community dance center," said her mom. "You're happy there?"

Mikayla broke into a grin, wiping away tears. "Yeah," she said. "It's great. Every time, we learn a new routine. . . ." She told them about the punch card, and Phillipa's philosophy, and the way she felt when she was dancing there.

"It sounds great," said her dad, wiping away another one of her tears.

Her mom smiled. "Can we come and watch you dance sometime?"

"It's nothing fancy or formal," said Mikayla. "But sure, you can come if you want. They have some seats in the back."

"We'd watch you dance anywhere," said her mom.

"We're proud of you," said her dad.

"Even now?" Mikayla asked.

"Yes," said her mom. "Especially now."

Aria looked down at her bracelet, expecting to feel the cool grace of the third charm on her wrist, but it wasn't there. She was surprised to feel a flicker of relief that it wasn't quite time to go yet. But she wondered what could possibly be left to do.

Mikayla got up and made her way down to the basement, and Aria trailed after. When the girls were alone, Aria flickered into sight, and began turning the gold trophies on Mikayla's wall pink and blue and green and purple.

Mikayla laughed and turned to see Aria there.

"I thought it might help," said Aria. "You know, take your mind off the gold and silver. . . ."

"It was you, wasn't it?" said Mikayla. "Somehow, you told Miss Annette, or . . ."

"I maybe tipped off Sara," said Aria, apologetically. "But I didn't know you'd actually tell your parents!"

"Have a little faith," teased Mikayla, shaking her head. "But maybe I needed the push. So, did you hear *everything*?" she asked. "Or do I need to catch you up to speed?"

Aria smiled bashfully. "I heard."

The two sat down on the floor, underneath what had been rows of gold trophies and were now rows of rainbows.

"So I guess that's that," said Mikayla. "No more Filigree. No more competitions, for now. Just dance."

"Are you happy?" asked Aria.

"I'm . . . relieved. Like a weight's been lifted, and I can breathe."

Aria nodded, knowingly. "Secrets are heavy," she said.

They both looked at the mirror. Aria studied the last clinging tendril of blue smoke around Mikayla's shoulders.

"You won't need me much longer," she said at last.

"You sound sad," said Mikayla.

Aria tried to smile. "Not at all!" she said, too cheerfully.

But staring at Mikayla's remaining blue smoke, Aria couldn't help but wonder what she was missing, and why she was so afraid of finding it.

The letter from Drexton came on Saturday.

It was sitting on the stoop, a shoe print on the envelope from where someone had stepped on it as they passed, obviously mistaking it for trash. But it wasn't trash. Aria could tell by the way the envelope made her feel just looking at it. It was important.

Aria hesitated. She understood, as soon as she saw it, what it was. What it *meant*.

This was the last step, the reason Mikayla's smoke hadn't disappeared.

The reason Aria was still there.

And then, out of nowhere, a thought occurred to Aria Blue.

Staring down at the letter, she realized that this was her chance. Her chance to avoid the unknown of what came next. To stay. To have a *life*. Mikayla didn't *know* the letter was coming. She wasn't expecting it. Only Aria knew that something was missing. If she didn't give the letter to Mikayla, then Aria wouldn't have to move on. She wouldn't be able to. And neither would Mikayla.

But . . . Mikayla *had* moved on. In almost every way. She'd found balance. She was happy.

Why shouldn't Aria be happy, too?

Her heart fluttered defiantly.

She knew it was wrong, to be afraid of the unknown. She knew it was breaking a rule — the most important one of all — to put herself before the girl she was supposed to help. But part of her still wanted to stay.

She could remain here, in this incredible city. She could see everything there was to see. . . .

But there were holes in her imagination, things she couldn't dream up, because she knew she couldn't magic them into being. Things like a family. A future. A normal life. Aria would never be a normal girl.

And deep down, she knew she wasn't meant to be one.

So she knelt down, picked up the letter, and slid it under the door.

chapter 25

MIKAYLA

The letter from Drexton came on Saturday.

It was sitting on the kitchen table, waiting in the spot where her dad's laptop usually was. Aria and Mikayla had just gotten back from a movie with Beth and Katie. It turned out Aria had never *been* to a movie theater before (something she confessed to Mikayla in a whisper as the previews started). It was crazy, the simple things she'd never done, and the joy she got out of doing them.

All the way back to Mikayla's house they'd chatted, Mikayla about the movie itself and Aria about how big the screen had been, and the peculiar buoyancy of popcorn. When they got to Mikayla's house, Aria seemed to see the envelope first. Mikayla followed her gaze and recognized the emblem: the two dancers woven together to form the *D* and *A* of Drexton Academy. Mikayla came to an abrupt stop.

Mikayla's mom was standing beside the table, waiting.

"It came today," she said. "I hope you'll forgive me, I snuck a peek."

Mikayla looked from her mom to Aria to the letter on the table, and then she picked it up with nervous fingers, and began to read aloud.

"Dear Mikayla Stevens," she read, voice trembling, "Congratulations. The Admissions Committee at Drexton Academy would like to offer you a place . . ."

Mikayla stopped reading and looked up.

"I don't understand," she said. "It must be a mistake."

"It's not," said her mom. "I called Drexton, and apparently one of their talent scouts has a daughter who takes classes at the Community Dance Center. She saw you dance."

Mikayla smiled sadly, and laughed.

"What is it?" asked her mom.

"Miss Annette used to say that someone important was *always* watching. I guess she was right." She looked at her mom. "What am I supposed to do?"

"It's your choice," said her mom. "It has to be your choice."

Mikayla looked down at the paper in her hand. For a second, she felt once again like the girl who only wanted to be gold. It was hard enough to move past something when you'd lost. But it was even harder to walk away from something when you'd *won*.

Even if it wasn't what you wanted anymore.

The silence in the room grew heavy.

And then Mikayla closed her eyes and set the letter back on the table. She put her hand over it, ran her fingers over the emblem embossed on the paper.

And then she pushed it away.

"I love to dance," she said. "But I don't want to eat and sleep and breathe dance." She smiled. "I want to eat and sleep and breathe *and* dance. It's an honor to be offered a place, but it's not for me. Not right now."

Mikayla's mom brought a hand to her shoulder and squeezed. "Okay, then."

"Okay," Mikayla echoed. And for the first time in ages, the word was true.

Then, out of the corner of her eye, she saw Aria slip through the front door and onto the porch.

Mikayla hurried after, afraid the girl would just disappear from her life as easily as she had first appeared. But she found her standing on the front step looking down at her charm bracelet, where a third feather charm now glinted in the afternoon light.

"Hey," said Mikayla.

"Hey," said Aria.

For an instant, she seemed . . . insubstantial, like Mikayla could put her hand right through her. But when she reached out and touched the angel's arm, it was solid, still there.

"I thought of another place to take you," said Mikayla. "We can go tomorrow after dance. There's a great cafe with these amazing cookies, and —"

"I'm sorry," said Aria gently. "I don't think I'll be able to come with you."

"Oh," said Mikayla. There was a moment of sad silence — they both knew what the feather charm meant — but then Mikayla said, "Can you stay for dinner?"

And to her relief, Aria burst into a smile. She pulled a piece of folded paper from her pocket, and held it up for Mikayla to see. It was titled *Aria Blue's Things to Do*, and there in the middle of the page, amid a sea of checked-off tasks, many of them big and exciting, was a simple desire that made Mikayla's heart twist.

Eat dinner with a family, it said.

"I'd love to," said Aria.

And Mikayla was glad that, for once, she could be the one helping.

chapter 26

ARIA

"Come on, give it back," said Mikayla, wresting a tennis ball from Chow's mouth. "Let go."

They were sitting on her back steps after dinner — after the best and only home-cooked meal that Aria had ever had — tossing the ball into the garden for the excitable dog. It was cool, but not too cold, and the sunset was leaving bright streaks of color across the sky. Aria gazed up at it, trying to convince herself that it was a gift, this last sunset. Trying not to think that word: *last*.

Then Aria's gaze drifted down to her charm bracelet. Along with the third and final feather, she'd felt something else settle over her, a simple, solid certainty that she was done here. That it was time to go.

Go where? she wondered to herself, a thread of panic weaving through the calm. She was always telling the girls she helped to look forward, to not be afraid of change. Now she had to take her own advice.

Mikayla wrapped her arm around Aria's shoulders, and the two sat there for a moment in silence.

Aria's shadow fidgeted beneath her. "I better get going," she said at last.

Mikayla started to nod and then bounced to her feet, eyes bright with an idea.

"Wait!" she said, turning to go inside. "Stay here. I have something for you!"

Before Aria could say anything, the girl was gone. She got slowly to her feet, and stretched, and waited.

Suddenly, though, Aria's shadow began to glow. And as it filled with impossible light, she could see the hint of wings.

A strange panic filled her chest.

Mikayla wasn't back yet, but there was something about the pulse of light, something unspoken, that told her it would be okay. This wasn't an end. Just another step. Her shadow knew best. It always did. So she took a breath, and looked up at the sky one last time, just in case, and stepped into the light.

· · ·

One moment Aria was surrounded by white, and the next moment she found herself standing in a girl's bedroom. She recognized it at once. The walls had been painted purple since her last visit, and were now covered in art and photos. Gabby was sitting cross-legged on the bed, hunched over homework, a thin stream of music pouring from the headphones around her neck. She was singing along softly. Her voice was lovely as always.

Aria smiled. "Hi," she said.

But Gabby didn't look up.

Aria frowned, realizing that Gabby couldn't see her. Which was weird, because she could still see herself. She was all there, from her green sweater to her blue tights down to her pink-laced shoes. But when she brought her hand to the corner of the bed, it went right through.

It didn't make sense. Her shadow had sent her, so she knew she was supposed to be here. But if not for Gabby, then for whom?

And then Aria understood.

This trip was for *her*.

One last look.

Someone knocked on the doorframe. A lanky teenage boy. Gabby's older brother, Marco.

He had a cane in one hand and was clearly tired, but he looked much better. Stronger. The color was in his cheeks and his eyes were bright. He looked right through Aria at his sister.

"Hey, Gabs," he said. "Dinner."

Gabby nodded. She tossed the headphones onto the pile of homework and got up, walking within inches of Aria.

Aria noticed that her laces were purple.

"Bye, Gabby," she said, right before the girl vanished through the door. To her surprise, Gabby stopped, and turned back. She couldn't have heard her, but her eyes still hovered on the air near Aria's head.

"What is it?" asked Marco.

"Nothing," said Gabby after a moment. "I just thought I heard something."

"Must be ghosts," said Marco, with a teasing stomp of his foot.

Gabby grinned, and gave him a playful shove toward the kitchen. She cast one last glance back. "Must be," she whispered. And then she was gone.

Aria smiled after her.

The shadow at her feet began to glow again.

"Okay," said Aria, looking down. As she stepped into the light, she had a feeling she knew where it would take her next.

There was a campfire in the backyard.

A handful of girls huddled around it, elbow to elbow as they toasted marshmallows on metal skewers and traded stories. It was dark, but Aria could see the outline of the trampoline behind them. She recognized Ginny and Elle, and Lily.

And there, blond hair pulled into a ponytail, was Caroline.

Caroline tilted her head back, and so did Aria. It was a clear night, and unlike in the city, here the sky was full of stars. Aria smiled, and one shot across the sky.

Caroline broke into a grin. "Did you see that?" she asked, but the girls had been staring down at the fire, and looked up too late. She was met by a chorus of *no* and *see what*.

"A shooting star." Caroline pulled her marshmallow from its stick and sandwiched it between two crackers along with some chocolate. It looked strange and wonderful and delicious, and Aria was secretly sad that she'd never gotten to try one. "Did you know that when you look up at the sky, you can see for almost twenty quadrillion miles?"

"Cool," said Ginny.

"Weird," said Elle.

"Random," said Lily, adding, "but still cool. Only you would know that."

"I didn't even know quadrillion was a word," said Ginny.

Elle squinted up. "That's a really long way."

"Yeah," said Caroline. "And all that empty space up there? It's not actually empty. It's full of stuff we just can't see. Some of it we can't even explain . . ."

Aria smiled, and beneath her, the shadow began to glow again with light.

Aria expected to find herself back in front of Mikayla's house. Instead, she wasn't really anywhere. She was standing in an empty place, everything blank like the screen before a movie started. Then, instead of going backward, or staying put, time began to roll *forward*.

Of course. Because she wouldn't be there to see it.

Aria stood still as Mikayla's future unfolded around her, not solid but ghostly as smoke, the images twisting into one another, tangling.

Aria saw Mikayla at the Community Dance Center, but she wasn't alone. Beth and Katie were with her, all of them breathless from dance and laughter.

She saw Mikayla going to movies, and school parties, riding her bike with Alex, and drawing with Katie, and playing tennis with Beth. She saw her tossing the ball for Chow and reading on the front stoop.

She saw her packing up the trophies and the rest of the house, saw her in a new apartment — smaller, but still home. She saw her tacking the now battered list of goals up on the new wall, old lines crossed out, new ones added.

She saw her, taller now, stretched out in Central Park, listening to music, with Alex by her side.

And Aria saw Mikayla *dancing*. Threaded through every memory of a life not yet lived, she watched the girl made of gold fall back in love with dance.

The last thing Aria saw wasn't from months or years in the future. It was probably only a few minutes ahead of now. She saw Mikayla standing in her backyard alone, staring at the place where Aria once stood. She saw her turn and go inside, through the house and out the front door. She saw her take a deep breath and then turn to Alex next door, working on his bike. Saw her smile, and lean across the fence, and say, "Hey, stranger. Still up for that ride?"

. . .

The light flared again, and Aria found herself back in Mikayla's yard as if nothing had changed.

And seconds later, Mikayla came through the door. "Good," she said. "You're still here."

Aria nodded. "I'm still here."

Mikayla hopped down the steps with something hidden behind her back. "You should have these," she said, revealing the gift: a pair of iridescent wings, the very same ones from Mikayla's dance costume.

The air caught in Aria's chest, and she smiled so wide that the setting sun grew brighter.

Aria took the wings, and slipped the straps on.

They were nearly weightless, but as they settled on her shoulders and against her back, they *changed*. The wings became heavier, more substantial. And when she looked down at her shadow, there they were, but they were different. The flimsy translucent material was gone, replaced by something that glowed with bluish light. The wings now arched gracefully over her shoulders and ended near her palms in feathered tips.

They weren't the stuff of costumes anymore.

They were real.

And they were *Aria's*.

It was better than anything she could have hoped for. It was the best gift. The best good-bye.

"Thank you," she said, still beaming.

"You've earned them," said Mikayla.

A breeze blew through, and the silver charms on her bracelet jingled faintly, like wind chimes.

"I wish you didn't have to go," said Mikayla.

Moments earlier, she would have said, "Me too," but now, after everything she'd seen, she said, "Don't worry. You're going to be amazing. Trust me."

"So will you," Mikayla said.

Aria took a deep breath and looked down at her shadow. The wings shimmered and then extended, stretched like welcoming arms toward her.

"Okay," she said to the angel's shadow. "I'm ready."

She tapped her shoe, and the shadow flared white.

Aria closed her eyes.

Endings are beginnings, she told herself.

And then she heard a flutter of wings, and stepped forward into the light.

ABOUT THE AUTHOR

Victoria Schwab is the acclaimed author of several novels for young adults and adults, including *The Archived* and *Vicious*. Everyday Angel is her first series for middle-grade readers. Victoria lives in Nashville, but she can be found haunting Paris streets and trudging up English hillsides. Usually, she's tucked in the corner of a coffee shop, dreaming up stories. Visit her online at www.victoriaschwab.com.

Read on to find out how Aria's story started. . . .

The lobby was filled with people, some in white coats, moving briskly, and some in regular clothes, slumped in chairs. Aria scanned the crowd, but she didn't see any smoke.

"Good afternoon," said a woman behind the desk. "How can I help you?"

Aria approached the desk. "I'm just trying to find someone."

"Who are you looking for?" asked the woman.

"Oh, I don't know," said Aria brightly. "I haven't found them yet." The woman frowned, but before she could say anything, Aria smiled and added, "Don't worry. I'll know them when I see them."

And with that she set off down the hall on the left.

She explored two floors in search of the smoke — scanning halls, peering through windows and around doors — until she stumbled upon a common room. Several children clustered around a TV, a few others sat around a table with a puzzle, but it was the boy by the window who caught her eye.

He was pale and blond and wreathed in smoke.

The dark plumes hung around him like a cloud as he stared out the window. But as Aria drew closer, she frowned.

His smoke was the wrong color. Aria was meant to find *blue* smoke. But the cloud circling the boy's shoulders was a dark, bruised purple. Almost black.

He was definitely marked, but not for Aria.

"Henry," said a voice, and the boy by the window looked up as a nurse carried a cup of water over to his wheelchair.

Aria wondered why Henry was here, and why he was shrouded in such a grim cloud. She looked around, searching for someone like her, maybe someone with a charm bracelet to match that particular shade of purple-black smoke. But no one stood out. In fact, Aria was the only person in the common room who didn't look like she belonged there.

Until another girl came in. She was about Aria's size, with warm, tan skin and rich, dark hair. But what caught Aria's attention wasn't the girl's skin or her hair or the notebook she was clutching to her chest. It was the blue smoke swirling around her shoulders.

Smoke the exact same color as Aria's bracelet.

The girl didn't seem *sick*, not like the other kids in the common room. But that didn't surprise Aria. After all, the smoke had nothing to do with sickness. It marked a person only if Aria could help them, and she couldn't help sickness. She wasn't a healer. (She didn't even know if those existed.) Aria was just . . . Aria. And whatever was wrong with the blue smoke girl, Aria was pretty sure she wouldn't figure it out by standing there. Plus she was beginning to feel awkward about staring. So she took a deep breath, walked up to the girl on the couch, and said hello.

Read on for a sneak peek at Aria's second mission. . . .

Second
Chances

VICTORIA SCHWAB
everyday
angel

SCHOLASTIC

Aria watched Caroline walk away from her. She didn't understand what was going on. Who was Lily Pierce? And what
had Caroline done to make her mad? Was the whole school
really ignoring Caroline just because one girl told them to?

Her thoughts swirled like Caroline's smoke. She looked
down at her black laces. She wished they were still purple. She
was *sure* she'd be able to think better if they were purple.

She tapped her shoe a few times. And then she got an idea.

Aria ducked into the bathroom. When she entered a
stall, she saw a message scribbled on the wall:

Caroline Mason is a waste of space.

Something fluttered in Aria's chest, a sensation she'd
never felt before, and it took her a moment to realize what it

was: *anger*. She brought her fingertips to the message, and it erased itself.

And then, Aria erased *herself*.

Aria didn't *like* being invisible. It certainly came in handy, but it always left her feeling . . . less than real. Still, if she was going to help Caroline, she needed to understand exactly what was going on, and it seemed like the best way to do that was to watch what Caroline's life was like without Aria in it.

Aria stepped out of the stall, and then she went in search of Caroline.

She caught sight of the blue smoke just as Caroline was reaching her last class, art. Aria slipped through the door behind her.

Caroline took her seat, and Aria stood beside her, hoping that even if she couldn't see her there, Caroline might feel a little less alone.

"Good afternoon, class," said the art teacher. "It's such a lovely day. I thought we could go outside and draw."

A murmur of approval ran through the room as he began to take roll. "All right," he said when he was done. "The only one we're missing is Lily."

"I'm here, sir."

Caroline stiffened in her seat, and Aria turned to see Lily Pierce standing in the doorway.

"Sorry I'm late," she said, waving a note.

Aria's mouth hung open. Lily had black curls, and pale skin, and a dazzling smile. But it wasn't any of those things that made Aria gape. No, it was something no one else seemed to notice. Something no one else *could* see.

Lily Pierce was surrounded by bright blue smoke.

sometimes help comes from surprising places.

At a first glance, Aria seems like your average twelve-year-old girl. She has coppery hair, colored shoelaces, and a passion for cupcakes. But Aria has a secret: She's a real-life guardian angel, and she's been sent here to earn her wings. In order to do that, she'll have to help out three different girls with very real troubles…